King of New York

Lock Down Publications and Ca$h
Presents

King of New York
A Novel by *T.J. Edwards*

Lock Down Publications
P.O. Box 870494
Mesquite, Tx 75187

Visit our website @
www.lockdownpublications.com

Lock Down Publications
Like our page on Facebook: Lock Down Publications @
www.facebook.com/lockdownpublications.ldp
Cover design and layout by: **Dynasty Cover Me**
Book interior design by: **Shawn Walker**
Edited by: **Sunny Giovanni**

Stay Connected with Us!

Text **LOCKDOWN** to 22828 to stay up-to-date with new releases, sneak peaks, contests and more…
Thank you.

DEDICATIONS

Man, what a Wife!!! You are simply the Truth!!! I love you so freaking much. You hold me down like no other. I am in such awe of you, Boo!!! I know that we go through our ups and downs, but I can never deny how happy I am with you through it all. There is nobody like my Jelissa Shanté !!! You come from me!!! My rib! You mean more than this world to me. I belong to you. I submit to you with all that I am, Mommas. Long as I'm breathing you won't have to worry about anything! Whatever you want, is yours, first. You're my spoiled lil' Baby-girl and that's how I wanna keep it. Long as we stay aligned under CHRIST we won't have any worries. I got you!!! Thank you for entrusting me to lead. I love you with my whole heart.

To LDP's number one rida, HELENE YOUNG! Thank you for all of your support. Every time a book drops, you are the first to grab it with no hesitation. Queen, your loyalty is unmatched. We truly honor and appreciate your undying devotion to LDP! Without true, die-hard supporters like you, us authors wouldn't survive in this competitive industry! Your advice to add more romance inspired this series! Thank you Queen!Love!

To Ca$h & Shawn: Thank you for your continued hard work and dedication to LDP. For doing all you can to advance as well as improve the company. Thank you for giving me a positive way to provide for my family. LDP

#LDP
#TheGameIsOurs

T.J. EDWRDS

Chapter 1
Tristian

I made another revolution around my brother, Showbiz's, 911 GT3 Porsche, with a sly smile on my face. The sun beamed off the top of my low-cut, deep waves. My usual light caramel complexion had darkened to the hue of a golden brown. The humidity was something fierce. I dabbed at the sweat that peppered along my forehead with a handkerchief, took the strap of my suitcase off my shoulder, opened the backdoor to his whip, and tossed it on the seat before sliding into the passenger's seat. They were all white, and soft leather. "Oh, so this how you doing it now, huh?" I looked over at him and nodded.

Showbiz leaned across the console and shook up with me. He was my older half-brother. He had me by three years. I say half because we had the same Cuban father but different mothers. My mother, Debra, was African American. She was 5'7", and about 130 pounds. While Showbiz's mother was Cuban, like our father, she was also 5'5" and weighed nearly the same as my mother. Though we were only paternal brothers, we saw ourselves as full-blooded ones. Showbiz had been in my life ever since I'd come out of my mother's womb.

He smiled at me, pulled out of John F. Kennedy Airport's parking lot, and dropped the hard top to the Porsche. The sun made its presence felt right away. "Kid, I already told you what it was. I told you I wasn't copping one of these joints until I was ten bricks and five hundred thousand to the good. Well, thanks to our old man, I damn near doubled that over the lil' ten days that you was away on Spring Break. The whip is courtesy of one of Pop's plugs. I ain't have to drop one red cent on this joker. How you love that?"

He sped out of the parking lot and in less than two minutes we were on the expressway. I was catching a cool breeze that I was loving. I was back home in the city of New York. I felt good. Even the pollution in the air smelled good to me. I'd only been away in Cancun, Mexico for ten days but it felt like ten months. The entire time I'd been down there, there had been so many security precautions that it made it basically impossible to enjoy my vacation. The cartels were making it a habit of kidnapping tourists and demanding a ransom. If the ransom was not paid, then they were beheading their captives and leaving them on the side of the road to be discovered. Where I'd been vacationing had been a hot spot for the act. So, the entire time I felt out of bounds and on edge. It felt good to be back where I knew the streets and the city like the back of my hand.

"Yo, this what's up though. You already know once I get my shit together I gotta one up you with something a lil' more foreign and a tad hotter. It ain't sweet; you already know that," I reminded him and looked over my shoulder to my sleeping nephew.

His name was Maine. He had earbuds in his ears that were hooked up to his iPad. The Ray Ban's on his face had slipped down his nose a bit. His neck was bent at an awkward angle. I could hear him snoring. I reached over my seat, getting ready to wake him up. I'd missed him.

Showbiz grabbed my wrist and pulled it back. "Hell nall, lil' bruh. Leave his lil' ass sleep for a minute. Fa real. He been taking me through one for the last two days. I need a mini break." He shook his head, looking into his rearview mirror at my six-year-old nephew who was his spitting image.

Both were golden brown, with long curly hair that was kept mainly in a pony tail. Both had light brown eyes. Eyes that had been passed down through our father, Chico's, genes. Not only did my brother and nephew have them but so did me and my sister, Brooklyn.

Showbiz's baby mother, Carmalita had died while giving birth to Maine. Carmalita had been Showbiz's first love. Prior to her having Maine, she and Showbiz had been a part of one another ever since they were five years old. At her funeral had been the only time I'd witnessed my brother crying as a man. I think it was because of her death that he'd become so heartless, and more of a loose cannon that he'd ever been prior to her passing. Maine was his world. While he was being born, my brother was being held in the county jail on a probation violation. So, after Carmalita passed away, her sister, Ebony, was given sole custody of Maine for the first five and a half years of his life because my brother had been in and out of prison.

He recently had been given sole custody of Maine, and I could tell that it was taking some getting used to. Showbiz was a street nigga. He was bred by the Harlem River Houses which was a cut-throat housing projects in Harlem, New York. He ran his own operation of dope boy savages.

"Yo, it's good, but before I get out the whip, I want chop it up with my nephew, man. I ain't seen his lil' ass in almost two weeks. I missed him. I'm hoping you'll let him rollout to Jamaica with me and Kalani next month. It's only for a week but that should be a nice amount of bonding time for me and him. What you think?"

Showbiz shrugged. "Shid, it's good with me. I just gotta run it by Tori. You know how overprotective she is about lil' homey. She be acting like she popped him out and shit. So long as she ain't gon' give me a headache about it, then it's good. I need a break anyway." He switched lanes and stepped on the accelerator. The Porsche sped forward with a low-pitched hum.

I activated the massage device on my seat and let it back a lil' bit with my eyes closed. The cool wind blew into my face, and I couldn't help smiling. I was so happy to be home. "How many months is Tori now?" I asked, opening my eyes and looking over at him.

Showbiz and Tori had hooked up a year after Carmalita had passed away. She'd grown up in the same projects with my brother. Though I didn't know much about her I felt that she was good for him. My brother was a hot head and she seemed to be the only one that could calm him down and talk some sense into him. I could tell that he really cared about her too.

Even though Showbiz was a bit of a hoe, that nigga had all types of bad bitches all over New York and beyond. It was him that made me get my hit list of pussy up to par. For as long as I could remember

I'd always looked up to my brother, even though we had different viewpoints on life. He saw himself being the King of the Underworld. A drug lord that had a thousand killas that followed behind him and praised him like a god. He wanted to be a more iconic version of our father who was a legend in his own right both in the States and in Cuba. Showbiz had a knack for the drug trade. He, like myself, was a supreme hustler and dope boy. All he saw was the dirty side of things.

Me? I wanted to be bigger than New York. I wanted to be one of the most influential and successful businessmen that New York or the world had ever seen. I wanted to have successful businesses all over the Unites states along with property. For me, the drug trade was a spring to launch me onto greener pastures. I wanted to contribute long-lasting wealth to my family and children whenever I chose to bring them into the world. That's why with every move I made in the game there was always a reason for it. It was imperative that I stayed three moves ahead at all times.

Showbiz shook his head and laughed to himself. "She's six months right now. I can't wait until she have our little girl, man. It seem like ever since she been pregnant, she been a whole other person. Shit getting old." He slowed down to honor a red light, then made a right and sped down West 155th Street.

"That's why I ain't trying to pop my seed until I'm ready for all of that. I'm one semester away from getting my Bachelors of Science degree in Business Management. This my fourth year. I can't wait until

I can see that paperwork. That's when life really gon' start for the kid, nah'mean?"

Showbiz waved me off and shook his head. "I'm proud of you, lil' bruh, but fuck all of that." He wiped his mouth. "I ain't ever had the patience for all of that school shit. I love fast money. I love flexing on nigga's right now. I love fucking niggas' bitches behind they back and sending them back home with my dick on they breath, son. I love riding foreign and staying in a fucking min- mansion right now. I can't wait like you, kid. I wish I could, but that shit ain't in me. I think it's where our different mother's come into play. I wanna be just like Pops on every level, but greater. Whereas you, you see shit differently."

I nodded. "I just want that generational wealth, Showbiz. Even though our family is killing the game right now, I know it won't last forever. Whenever it all falls I wanna be able to keep us living the lives that we've become accustomed to. Moms, Pops, our children, and the women in our lives deserve at least that. Nah'mean?"

Showbiz nodded. "Like I said, we see shit differently. I think the club that I'm opening in mom's name is gon' be a hit. I got some of the baddest bitches on the east coast that's ready to shake they ass in there. I'm talking hoes so thick that it make mufuckas uncomfortable like that nigga Drake said. Once that bitch get to popping like I know it will, then I'ma open another one, and so forth and so on."

"Yo, and I guess I'm gon' be the one to teach you about the books and how to properly run that joint so you can maximize your profits and become an elite businessman all around the board, huh?" I laughed.

He bumped fists with me. "You already know, 'cuz all that shit is foreign to me." Before he pulled his fist back, he lowered his eyes and scrunched his bushy eyebrows. "I knew I was gon' run into this bitch nigga before the week was out." He reached under his seat and placed a .45 automatic on his lap. As the Porsche cruised into Holcombe Rucker Park, he cocked the weapon and sucked his teeth loudly. "Look, Tristian, I'm about to go and holla at this nigga, Flex. I fronted him two birds a month ago, and this nigga been ducking me ever since. He ain't returning my text, calls, or none of that shit so you already know what it is. Here." He grabbed another .45 from his glovebox and handed it to me.

I pulled my seat all the way up, bucked my eyes and felt my heartbeats pounding in my chest. It never seemed to fail. Majority of the times I was out rolling with my brother there was always some sort of beef that took place. It was crazy. "Bruh, you finna do this shit with Maine in the car?"

I looked out and saw two black on black Cadillac Escalades with gold rims parked in the parking lot. Outside of them were four dudes. Three were talking on their cell phones. These must've been Flex's homeboys. Flex himself was the only one not talking on a cell phone. He was on one knee with a rag in his hand, shining the right front rim of one of the trucks.

"My lil' nigga need to get used to how his old man gets down anyway. That goon shit is in his blood. This is the life he was born into." Showbiz retorted, pulling the Porsche into a parking space. He placed the .45 into the small of his back and slid gloves onto his hands.

I looked to my right at the basketball courts. There were two young boys about the age of fourteen and fifteen playing one on one. They were talking smack to each other. While at the other end of the courts across the half-court mark were three girls jumping double-dutch. I didn't like the set up for what Show Biz was planning. There were too many kids around. Not to mention my nephew Maine. I looked over my shoulder at him and confirmed that he was still sleeping. He was.

"Kid, I'm about to go out here and see what's good with my scratch. If this nigga ain't talking right, I'ma drop him where he stands. Word is bond." He threw open the suicide door and jumped out of the whip with a scowl on his face.

I put the .45 on my hip and looked in the rearview mirror as he walked up to Flex with his arms spread out like a lower-case T. Flex stood up and the group of men took a few steps back as if they didn't want to be involved. At least that's the impression I got in the beginning.

I wanted to get out and stand behind my brother, but we'd been in this type of position before. When Showbiz felt strongly about something there was nothing that anybody could do to stop him. He was a loose cannon and had told me time and time again to never try and save a nigga that he felt had wronged him, to only stand back and let him handle his business. So, that's what I was doing, even though something was nagging at me to go against his usual orders. I just didn't feel right.

I looked over and saw him step into Flex's face. His hand went under his shirt and I knew it was about to go down. I looked back toward the basketball courts and knew that if a big shootout started that those lil' kids would be in the line of fire. Sweat appeared on my forehead. I wiped it away and swallowed. Before I could think to stop myself, I opened the passenger's door and stepped foot on the gravel of the parking lot.

Showbiz upped his pistol and slammed it under Flex's chin. He picked him up by the neck and slammed him to the concrete with his pistol still tucked strongly under his chin, against his neck. "Bitch nigga, you gon' pay me my muthafucking money or the next time I see you I'ma slump you and these pussies you roll with. That's my word." He snapped with the hammer to the .45 cocked backward.

I stepped into the gateway of the courts. "Aye! Say, shorties, why don't y'all get up out of here before something bad happen?" I yelled at them.

The little boys waved me off and kept on playing ball. The little girls dropped the rope and began to jog in my direction. They were about a hundred feet away when I looked over my shoulder and saw Showbiz walking away from Flex and his niggas.

He opened the door to his Porsche and Flex ran to the driver's side of one of the trucks, opened the door, and came out of it with two .9 millimeters. The sun reflected off the chrome. "Aye, bitch nigga!" He hollered.

"Showbiz! Watch out, big bruh!" I upped the .45, and before I could let loose a slug, Flex started to bussing with both guns. *Boom. Boom. Boom.* His bullets slammed into my brother's back, knocking him into the Porsche, and Flex kept on bussing.

I sent three slugs in his direction. *Boom. Boom. Boom.* I saw Showbiz run across the front of his car before kneeling on the opposite side of his Porsche. He started to shoot at Flex and his men.

The heavy scent of gun powder entered the air. It sounded like the fourth of July. One of Flex's men cocked a Tech .9 and started to chop up my brother's whip, hiding behind his truck. While his guys jumped in the SUV and remained there, Showbiz continued to buss over the Porsche's body. All the chaos must've awakened Maine. He pulled the earbuds out of his ears and looked around in a frenzy as bullets riddled the body of the Porsche, Swiss Cheesing it. I saw Showbiz open the passenger's door that he was ducked behind, grab Maine's leg and pull him out alongside him.

I was ducked along the fence with the little girls laid out on their stomachs beside me. They were screaming loudly, I guessed scared out of their minds. The one with the Tech .9 emptied his clip, slammed another into the magazine and ran toward the basketball courts where we were, in a haste. I leveled my .45 and got ready to squeeze the trigger to light his ass up when one of the little girls, no older than ten, jumped up and bumped the handle of my pistol with her head. Then she took off running in a panic. I aimed and fired three shots at him. Showbiz aimed his .45 and fired four in our direction. Flex fired two. There were so many bullets flying all over the place. The little girl took about six steps, and then her back filled with two holes. She fell to her knees.

I hustled to get over to her while shots continued to ring out. I stood up, ran, and jumped on top of her as the one with the Tech let four more slugs fly. Two of them slamming into my back, right below my right shoulder blade. The bullets felt like I was being stabbed with a flaming sword that was carving into me. The pain was so intense that I hollered and dropped my pistol. I made sure that my body was completely on top of the little girl to shield her from the shootout. I knew that she was already hit. I only prayed that her injuries weren't life-ending. I could hear her groaning in intense pain below me.

More shots were fired. Then there was the squealing of tires. Less than a minute later, there was complete silence. I could feel my blood pouring out of me at a rapid pace. I felt dizzy and extremely weak. I also noted that the little girl under me was no longer making any noise. That caused my heart to skip a beat.

Chapter 2

"Get up, Tristian! Come on man, before Twelve show up!" Showbiz hollered, pulling me off the little girl. His face was drenched in sweat. His eyes were watery. He was breathing as if he'd just sprinted for a half mile.

I allowed for him to get me up. I fell against him, feeling as if I was about to throw up from so much blood lost at one time. My vision was blurry. I looked down and saw the little girl. A puddle of blood had formed around her body. I broke away from Showbiz, kneeled and picked her up. "We gotta get her to a hospital, Biz. We can't let her die, bruh." The park was completely deserted with the exception of us three.

Showbiz wiped his mouth with the pistol in his hand. "Fuck that lil' bitch, man. They killed Maine. That fuck nigga Flex killed my son, Tristian. What am I gon' do?" he hollered gritting teeth.

I felt the tears sliding down my cheeks. I imagined my nephew losing his life and it made me sick to my stomach. I cradled the little girl and started to make my way toward the opening of the gate with her. I was on wobbly legs. I felt like I was about to faint at any second. My entire back was saturated in blood. I could feel the holes in my back leaking like a broken faucet. As weak as I felt, I knew that I had to get this child into the Porsche, so we could get her to the hospital. I didn't know if she was alive or dead, but in my opinion none of it should have happened. Showbiz and I should have never been there when we were. I felt obligated to do everything that I could for this child.

Showbiz jogged alongside me. "Did you hear what I said, Tristian? Maine is dead. My fucking son is dead!" He ran ahead and opened the passenger's door for me.

I staggered with the little girl, got her to the car, and before I lowered her into the backseat I saw that Maine was already there, lying flat on his back with blood running out of a big hole on the side of his head. Half of his skull was missing. I swallowed and climbed into the front passenger's seat with the little girl still in my arms. I was so dizzy that I could barely keep my eyes open.

Showbiz jumped into the Porsche, threw it into gear and pulled out of the parking lot. "My son, man. How could this happen? I'ma kill them Harlem niggas." He rubbed at the holes in his shirt. I could see his bulletproof vest through the material. Ever since he'd been twelve years old my brother had worn a bulletproof vest. Wearing a vest had saved his life on numerous occasions.

My eyes rolled into the back of my head. I lost consciousness for what seemed like two minutes, but it had only been twenty seconds before I regained it. "Get us to Mount Sinai, Biz. Hurry up or we gon' die too," were the last words I said before I passed out, holding the child as tight to my chest as I could.

* * *

I didn't wake up until later that night. That was after my surgery. The surgeon had pulled two bullets out of my back. In addition to that I'd gotten a blood transfusion. When I awoke I was handcuffed to the hospital bed, and there were two detectives waiting to talk to me. I already knew what it was. In New York, whenever you were the victim of a violent crime, especially a shooting, they wouldn't let you leave the hospital until you spoke with law enforcement or authorities. I was hip to the game, so I expected it.

As soon as the detectives saw that my eyes were opened, they rose from the couch and made their way over to my bedside with intimidating looks on their faces. One was a shorter, portly Black woman with short hair. The other a white man, about fifty years old, bald at the top of his head with hair around the sides.

He stepped forward with a pen and notebook. "Mr. Vega, nice to see you awake. You've been through a lot. Do you feel as if you're conscious enough to talk?"

I adjusted my pillow and laid my head back on it. I felt kind of high from the morphine that they'd pumped into me during my surgery. My throat was dry, and I felt the need to cough. "I ain't got nothing to say to y'all. I need to call my lawyer. That's it, that's all."

The Black woman smiled. "Sir, I'm Detective James. We're just here to investigate what took place at Rucker Park early this day. We're not here to persecute you in any way. It's just that you were not the only victim. There was also a little girl that was hit. A little girl whose blood was all over you when you were admitted. And yours was all over her as well.

Care to explain?" She pulled out her notepad and looked me in the eye.

"Look, Miss, whatever your name is. I ain't got shit to say to either one of you. I need to call my lawyer, and we can go from there. Now either give me a phone, or get the fuck out of my room, after you take these bitch ass handcuffs from my wrist!" I slid the cuffs up and down the pole I was confined to in anger.

"Will your lawyer explain to us why there was gunpowder residue on your right hand? Or whether or not you were the shooter that struck this child?" The white detective whose name tag read *Roberts* said to me.

There was a knock at the door. The nurse stuck her head in and stepped to the side. "I have a Mr. Shapiro here. He said he is the lawyer of Mr. Vega." She smiled weakly as Shapiro stepped into the room carrying his briefcase.

He was 5'8" with wavy black and gray hair. Jewish. He'd been the attorney for our family for as long as I could remember, and he was damn good at his job too. He'd helped both my brother and father beat numerous murder cases and allegations. He was well respected by me.

He came in and stepped in front of the detectives, blocking my view of them. "Do you have any reason to have placed Mr. Vega in handcuffs? He is a victim! I demand you to take them off of him right this instant or I will slap a cruelty and an abuse of power charges on the both of you so quick that you'll be placed on desk duty for the next six months until our suit is resolved in a manner that not only appeases my client but any of the other potential victims that you will victimize in this way in the future."

"Mr. Shapiro, your client is a suspect in an attempted homicide. There is a little girl down the hallway in the intensive care unit fighting for her life. If she passes away, he's on the hook for first degree murder." Detective Roberts spoke.

Mr. Shapiro stepped into his face after taking off his glasses. "You imbecile. Two forty-five rounds were taken out of Mr. Vega. There were also two forty-five rounds taken out of this little girl that you speak of. The same rounds were found in both victims. So, if we go by your logic, then this little girl should have also been placed in handcuffs, just like this victim right here." He pointed at me with his head.

The Black woman sighed. "Mr. Shapiro, your client had gunshot residue on his right hand, indicating that he's recently fired a weapon within the last twenty-four hours."

Shapiro opened his briefcase and handed them two sheets of paper apiece. "My client not only has a license to carry a firearm, but he also has multiple receipts for legal weapons that he's purchased and is well within his rights to do so. Donald Trump himself would kick you in the ass if he knew that you went around accusing and locking up every red-blooded American that fired legal weapons that they owned. Now, I'm going to give you a direct order to release my client from these binds or you can expect me to rain down fire on your heads the first thing Monday morning. Do it!" he shouted with his face beet red.

I had a slight smile on my face as they rushed to release me. I rubbed my wrists one at a time, looking from one on to the other. "If you'll leave my lawyer with your card, I'm sure we'll get back to you when it's convenient."

Detective James handed her card to Shapiro. "Have your client at our station Monday morning or there will be a warrant issued for his arrest." She looked over to me and frowned. "We'll see you real soon, Mr. Vega. You can count on that." Her and her partner left the room, closing the door behind them.

Shapiro ran his fingers through his wavy hair and placed his glasses back on his face. "You didn't tell them anything, did you?" He stepped to the side of the bed, grabbed a juice and stuck a straw into it. He handed it to me.

I shook my head. "I only told them I didn't have nothing to say. That I wanted to contact my attorney. That was it." I sipped from the straw. Cranberry juice took over my taste buds.

"That's good." He shook his head and exhaled. "Your nephew is deceased. Your father is irate, and they're right, if the little girl down the hallway dies we're going to have some serious trouble on our hands. This doesn't look good, and we can't have it coming out. Your father has decided to back Senator Jefferey Grant in his run for the Mayor of New York. He's putting a lot of political power behind him. During this campaign, you and Showbiz must stay in line. This mayoral position spells millions for the Vega family. I need for you guys to understand that." He pulled out his cell phone and sent a quick message.

I winced in pain. I felt like the morphine was wearing off or something. My back was killing me. "Trust me, I didn't want none this shit to fall like it did. I ain't have no say so in the matter. If I had, that baby wouldn't be down the hallway fighting for her life."

"Well, there's no use of crying over spilled milk. I'm going to get you out of here in a few hours. I'll see if they'll prescribe you some morphine tablets. If not, I'll use my own script to get them. So, get ready. I'll be back." He left the room.

I covered my face with my hands and tried to clear my head. I kept on replaying the shootout in my mind. The bullets flew in every direction. I saw the holes fill the little girl's back before I jumped on top of her. I saw Maine's lifeless body in the backseat of the Porsche. The tears that ran down my brother's cheeks. I felt like I could hear the thunderous sound of gunshots as clear as day. I squeezed my head harder and wanted to scream. Because of us, there was a little child fighting for her life. I felt lower than scum.

* * *

Shapiro wheeled me down the hallway on our way out of the hospital about four hours later. I'd popped two morphine tablets, so I was feeling breezy. The pain in my back was faint and manageable.

Nurses were scattered about down the narrow hallway. There was a voice that called out to a variety of doctors and ordered them to certain parts of the hospital from the PA system. The aroma of pepper-mints floated in the air.

When we got to the end of the hallway, alongside the waiting room, for the intensive care unit, I saw the same two detectives huddled in a corner talking to a caramel skinned, beautiful Black sista. Her eyes were bloodshot red. She dabbed at them with a Kleenex and hugged herself as she listened to what they had to say. Detective James held one of her hands. I took this to be the mother of the little girl right away.

I felt my heart skip a beat. I had to say something to her. There was an intense need for me to do so. "Shapiro, wheel me over to them, man," I ordered, about to get up out of the wheelchair.

He shook his head. "No, Tristian, we need to get out of here before they find a way to detain you. I still need to get a better understanding as to what took place yesterday, so I can build a defense."

I hopped out of the wheelchair and felt the sting-ing in my back become more prominent. I braced myself and made my way in the direction of the De-tectives and whom I presumed to be the little girl's mother.

Before I could get close enough to her, Detective James saw me and began to walk toward me. "I'm going to ask you to not bother the mother of the vic-tim, Mr. Vega." She held up a hand to halt me.

I side stepped her, braced my lower back and made my way toward the mother. "How is she doing? I need to know if she's okay."

She broke away from detective Roberts and frowned. "Are you the one?" She cried. "Are you the one that shot my innocent little girl?" She wiped tears away and stopped in front of me. Her nose was red, probably from the constant blowing of it. She had a prominent mole on the right side of her upper lip. With every word that she spoke, a dimple appeared on each cheek. I found her extremely attractive, even though it was the most inappropriate time to do so. She smelled of Jasmine perfume.

I shook my head. "No, I wasn't the shooter. I was the one that jumped on top of your daughter when the shooting began. I'd gotten there a second too late, and I regret it with all of my being." I winced in pain as I adjusted from one foot onto the other. Looking into her face I could tell that she was hurt beyond understanding. I wished in that moment that I could have removed that pain from her. No mother should have to feel what I imagined that she was feeling in that moment.

She sniffed and dabbed at her nostrils. "The detectives said that you were one of the shooters. That you had gunpowder residue on your hands. Is this true?" She stepped forward and looked up at me with questioning eyes.

In that moment I felt like walking her through everything as it happened. I could see that she was struggling to maintain her composure. She was shaking. Her lower lip twitching. I wanted to shelter her within my embrace.

"I-I-I mean, if you wanna just listen to what—"

Shapiro rushed in and separated us. "Okay, that's enough for now. I'm sure that you two will run into each other again. Ma'am, we are very sorry about what happened to your daughter. I assure you that

Mr. Vega did everything that he could to save your daughter. In fact, in the process, he himself was wounded."

"Yeah, look, I'm so sorry. I swear if I could have saved her I would have. I can only imagine what you're going through at this time. Can you please tell me how she's doing?"

She lowered her head and wiped more tears away from her cheeks. "I don't know. They won't tell me anything, but I can only imagine the worst because she's still in the intensive care unit. So far, they've said that one of the bullets is lodged in her spinal column. It's nearly impossible to remove without causing her some sort of long-term damage. She's just a little girl." She fell to her knees and cried with her face in her hands.

I dropped beside her and tried to put my arm around her shoulder.

She shrugged me off and stood up disgusted. "Don't you fucking touch me! Until I find out what role you played in all of this, you better stay as far away from my daughter as you can. You're the devil." She backed away from me.

Detective James placed her arm around her shoulder. "Come on now, Perjah, you have to be strong for Brittany. She needs your strength right now."

"Perjah." I whispered her name, so I could remember it. The little girl's name was Brittany. I'd make it my business to find out their last name. I needed to make amends for what had taken place with her child. *I needed to help Perjah in any way that I could*, I thought as Shapiro helped me to my feet and back into the wheelchair. "I swear I'ma do all that I can to make this right, Perjah. I'm so sorry for you and your daughter's pain."

She started to cry into Detective James' chest as Shapiro began to roll me out of the waiting area.

We rolled with my head down. My heart heavy with remorse and grief. Not only had I lost a nephew, but there was a chance that another child could lose her life. I felt as if I had the stomach flu.

"Shapiro, I want you to find out Perjah's last name, and that of Brittany. Nobody should have to experience the things that they are. Do you understand me?"

He nodded. "I'll do what I have to after I run this by your father. I think it's dangerous to be aligned with them in any way right now. You have your whole future ahead of you. One murder could damage you for life. I don't think you're getting that right now."

We were about twenty feet away from the exit when Flex appeared with two grimy looking men walking close behind. Both had long dreadlocks and mugs on their faces.

I lowered my head, shielding my face from their view as Shapiro rolled me past them and out of the double sliding doors. Before we were completely outside, I looked over my shoulder and saw Perjah run into Flex's awaiting arms. Then the door slid back into place and they were gone from my line of vision.

"Shapiro, did you just see those three men?" I looked up at him as the black Navigator pulled in front of us.

The driver got out and opened the back door for us. He helped Shapiro to get me inside of the backseat before Shapiro closed the door.

Shapiro got in the back with me and leaned over. "Yeah, I saw them. What about it?"

I shook my head. "Never mind. It's not important. Just find out as many things as you can about Perjah and Brittany, and we'll go from there." I watched the driver roll the wheelchair back into the hospital before getting back into the truck and pulling off.

Chapter 3

Showbiz stood over Maine's casket with dark sunglasses covering his eyes. He wiped away more than a few tears as they slid down his cheek. He shook his head and laid his hand on to Maine's chest. "I'm so sorry, son. I love you so much, baby." He broke into a fit of tears and knelt at the casket.

Behind Maine's coffin was his mother, Amelia. She wore a black Fendi dress with black eye makeup and black red-bottomed heels. In her hand was a microphone. She sang a slow, sad song in Spanish. I was only able to make out a few of the words.

We were in one of the church's that my father had seized when he'd come over from Havana, Cuba in the late nineties. The pastor of the church was more of a drug lord than a man of God. His name was Israel. He was my father's right-hand man. My father had taken ownership of fifty churches all over the five boroughs of New York. He used them as safe houses and distributing posts. Through their usage he was able to pump his heroin and cocaine throughout each borough of the Big Apple.

I stepped behind Showbiz and rubbed his back before placing my arm around his shoulder. It was eight days after the big event. Every time I'd tried to call him prior to my nephew's funeral he'd been unable to carry out a full conversation without breaking down. I knew that he was taking the loss of his first born very hard. "Man, I love you, Showbiz, and I'm here for you, big bruh. Whatever you need from me, consider it done." I hugged him and patted his shoulder.

He shook his head and looked down at Maine's body. "That nigga took my son from me, Tristian. I can't honor this shit, lil' bruh. Right now, I feel like I can wipe out that nigga's whole family, and I'd still be hurting, Kid. Maine was my last breathing version of Carmalita. What am I gon' do now?" He squeezed his eyelids together. Through the bright light shining from the ceiling of the church I was able to make them out. More tears slid down his cheeks. He slammed his fist onto the closed bottom portion of Maine's casket.

"Bruh, we gon' figure this out. Right now, just take some time out to grieve. It's the only thing we can do." I really didn't have the right words to say to him because, in my mind, I honestly felt like Maine's death was on him. It had been his choice to go out and pursue Flex. It had been his choice to step out of the car. He'd chosen to get into a disagreement with another man while Maine and myself were present. It seemed like one wrong decision after the next. If you asked me, Maine would have still had life in his body had Showbiz been smarter and less impulsive. But of course, I couldn't tell him that. He was already broken in the worst way. He'd lost his only son. I felt deeply for him. At the same time, I could not get Brittany off my mind either.

Ebony stepped behind us and cleared her throat. "Uh, excuse me, but you're not the only one that wishes to pay their last respects. If you two wouldn't mind stepping aside, that would be great." She rolled her eyes and crossed her arm in front of her chest.

Showbiz turned around with lightning speed and nudged me out of the way. "Bitch, I ain't got time for you right now. Don't bring all that drama and shit in this church. I ain't got no problem kicking yo' monkey ass out. Word up."

Ebony frowned. "Fuck you, Showbiz. You always got something slick or disrespectful to say. Why don't you step yo' ass to the side so everybody can say their goodbyes. It's too late to feel how you feeling. I should have never given yo' ass custody of my nephew. Now look where it got him."

Smack! Showbiz slapped her so hard that she fell to her knees. He picked her up by the hair and threw her toward the pews. "Get this ratchet ass bitch up out of here before she end up lying next to my baby." He snapped, signaling to our bodyguards.

Ebony slowly made her way to her feet. She looked over her shoulder at him with watery eyes, while at the same time her wrists were grabbed on each side by the guards. "I hate you, Showbiz. I never saw what my sister saw in you anyway. You killed my nephew, you negligent son of a bitch! You gon' get yours one of these days. I swear to God you are." The high yellow, green-eyed woman yelled as she was being led out of the church by force.

There were about twenty other close family members in the pews. None made a move to stop Showbiz or uttered a word. We were familiar with his temper. Felt that he had a right to do what he did. At least it's how I felt. On the flipside I could never blame him for how hot headed he was. I could be the same way at times.

My father stood up from the second row and made his way to the front of the small church with two armed bodyguards walking close behind him. He stepped up to me and kissed me on both cheeks. "Mijo, I need to speak with you and your brother first thing in the morning. Do you understand me?" He asked in his strong Cuban accent.

I nodded. "Yes, Pops, I'll be there." I hugged him and ended with kissing him on both cheeks.

My father was 5'10". He had light brown eyes that he'd passed on to all his children. He wore wavs that had specks of gray in them, a goatee, and always dressed in designer business suits unless he was on the beach or one of his yachts. He called me, Show-biz, and his other son, Miguel, Mijo. Mijo means *my son* in Spanish. I had a deep love and respect for my father. Even though he'd been knee deep in the dope game ever since I was a little boy, he'd always been a great father and provider for the family. He instilled hard work and dedication within me. That everything was earned and never given. To be given anything made one lazy and complacent. He'd said the harder you worked for something the more you appreciated it and was more apt to protect and cherish it.

He stepped up to Showbiz and leaned his head down so that he was looking into his eyes. "Mijo, what have I told you about the public abuse of women?"

Showbiz frowned and tried to jerk his head away, but my Pops held on to it. "Man, Pop, I ain't trying to hear that right now. That bitch was out of line. She already took me through way too much to get my son. Now she is talking crazy at his funeral. It's only so much I can take." He tried to jerk his head away again.

But my father kept it within his grasp. "Mijo, being impulsive will be your downfall. Emotions are meant to be controlled, not acted upon without thought. Look at the eyes of the women in the church. Do you see how much they fear you?" He stepped to the side, so my brother could scan the eyes of the remaining female family members.

I don't know what for sure it was that he really saw. But I noticed that in every direction that he looked, our female family members would either lower their heads or look off in another direction. I couldn't say for certain if it was from fear of him or just because.

Showbiz grunted and shrugged. "I don't give a fuck about none of that, Pop. My seed is laying in a coffin right now. I got a lot of street business on my mind. The last thing I'm concerned about is how these broads are eyeing me." He jerked away from my old man and looked into Maine's coffin once again. His glasses fell from his face on to Maine's chest.

My father laid his hand on his shoulder. "Grieve, Mijo, but tomorrow, you and your brother meet me at my estate in Bayside. We'll do brunch. I have some things that I need to run by the both of you in addition to this dilemma. I love you, Mijo. Both of you." He kissed us, then leaned down and kissed Maine on both cheeks. He said a silent prayer over him, crossed his casket with the sign of the crucifix, and then himself before leaving the church being followed by his two-armed Cuban guards. They were men that had grown up with him back in Havana— well trusted and proven.

* * *

After we buried my nephew and I said my final goodbyes I was exhausted. I made it home at seven o'clock that night. Before I could open the door to my brownstone, it was opened by Kalani.

Kalani was 5'4" and brown skinned with pure brown eyes. She had light freckles all over her face that made her look so unique and fine to me. She weighed about a hundred and twenty-five pounds. Kalani was one of the only women that I'd dated that I cared a great deal about. She was stomp-down, jazzy, often slick-tongued, brutally honest, and she loved me like no other woman ever had. We were raised together in the Red Hook Houses out in Brooklyn. She had been my high school sweetheart. We were the same age, and while in the tenth grade we'd had a pregnancy scare, she'd became pregnant with my child. When her mother found out, she beat her so bad that she'd lost our baby. I'd taken her in ever since then, and although our child had not made it to term, I still saw Kalani as my baby's mother. I held a deep respect and regard for her because of it. Even in most times when she got on my nerves.

She threw open the door and wrapped her arms around me. "Hey, boo. How was the funeral?" She hugged me tighter and looked up into my eyes.

I kissed her forehead and then her lips before breaking our embrace. "My brother taking it hard. He slapped Ebony's ass, and my old man got at him about it. But when I left, he was doing a lil' better. It's good." I closed and locked the door and made my way further inside my crib.

I saw that she had the big screen still on ESPN where I'd left it earlier that morning. My mind had been blown after finding out that LeBron was headed to the Los Angeles Lakers. He was my favorite basketball player and I was hoping that he came to play for the New York Knicks.

Kalani rushed ahead of me into the kitchen. She took my plate of food out of the refrigerator before removing the aluminum foil. Then she placed it into the microwave for ninety seconds. "That girl always causing drama. I never could stand her. Tell Showbiz to let me know if he want me to kick her ass. She deserve it for everything she done took him through to even get custody of his lil' boy." She shook her head. "I've missed you, baby. I don't understand why your brother wouldn't let me come to the funeral. I loved Maine just as much as anybody else." She poked out her bottom lip and popped back on her legs. Her hair was pulled back into a ponytail. She was dressed in sweatpants and a pink tank top on bare, pedicured feet.

I took off my suit jacket, my shirt and my bullet-proof vest that my father insisted on me wearing until we were able to have a sit down and talk about the Flex hit. My back was killing me once again. I made my way to the bathroom to get my Percocet. I had plans on popping two thirties. I was feening for them, even though prior to me being shot I'd never liked to fuck with pills 'n shit.

"Baby, he ain't let nobody that wasn't blood to Maine, come. My mother wasn't even there, and she was there when lil' homey was born. My brother just some type of way." I placed the two thirties on my tongue and filled my hand with water to chase them down. I couldn't wait until they kicked in. I was starting to feel nauseous.

Kalani stepped into the big bathroom and laid her face on my back. She kissed it and licked along my spine. "Every time I see these bandages it makes me sick. I wish I could kill the muthafuckas that did this to you." She kissed my bandages then peeled them off. It took her five minutes to sterilize my wounds and rebandage me.

I looked into her brown eyes and rubbed my nose against hers. "You always acting like you so hard. Ain't you supposed to be in there studying for your real estate test?" I backed her all the way against the wall, trailing my hands downward, and cuffed her rounded ass while sucking on her neck.

She purred and shuddered against me, rubbing her soft hands all over my shoulders and upper back. She looked so small compared to me, and I loved it. I sucked on her neck a little harder, just the way she liked it. "Un! I been studying while you were gone. I can take a lil' break. I'm good." She stepped on her tippy toes with her neck tilted, giving me more access.

I slid my hand down the front of her sweatpants, into her panties. My middle finger separated her pleasure lips. Her clit was already erect and slippery. I slid my finger into my mouth to taste her. I needed to take my mind off the funeral, Brittany, and Perjah. I just wanted to be somewhere else mentally. If only for an hour.

She pulled her sweatpants down and stepped out of them. Under them she was without underwear. Her brown thighs were thick, smooth, and looked good enough to eat. "I want you to taste me, Tristian. I been thinking about you all day long. I need you right now. I'm aching." She opened her sex lips, slid two fingers into herself, took them out and fed them to me.

I licked all around them before sucking them into my mouth. I dropped down to my knee and picked up her right thigh, placing it on my shoulder. I inhaled her womanly essence, then sucked her lips into my mouth loudly. I separated them with two fingers and licked up and down her bubble gum pink.

"Mmm, baby. Yes, it feel so good. Keep eating me like that." She grabbed the back of my head and forced me further between her thighs.

I trapped her clitoris with my lips and sucked it like a nipple while my tongue traced circles around it. I slid two fingers up her box and ran them in and out. My nose was right above her hole. I could smell her natural scent and it was driving me up the wall. There was nothing like the natural scent of a woman to me. I got to eating that box like I was starving— slurping her juices, swallowing them, and stabbing her with my tongue while my fingers dove in and out of her. Her essence dripped from my wrist and ran down my forearm.

She bucked into my face. Her eyes rolled into the back of her head before the shaking began. "I'm cumming, bae. Bae. Bae. I'm cumming so hard!" She screamed, forcing my face into her slit with brute strength.

I grabbed a hold of her ass cheeks and swallowed everything that she skeeted out of her. She dropped and pulled my boxers from me, stroking my manhood. Her tongue ran across her lips. She looked at the head hungrily, then sucked it into her mouth, licking around it, then up and down the stalk. She took me deep. Her jaws hollowed as she sucked loudly.

I grabbed a hand full of her hair and guided her. It felt so good. She nipped at my head with her teeth, causing my toes to curl. I bit into my bottom lip, humping forward into her hot mouth. There was nothing like watching a dime suck all over my mans down low. Kalani was bad. Sometimes watching her do her thing to me caused me to cum harder than when we were fucking. That's not saying that her pussy wasn't on point, because it most definitely was.

I snatched her up by the hair and bent her over the sink in the bathroom and smacked that fat ass one time real hard before running my head up and down her wet slit. She reached under herself and spread the lips wide, anticipating my intrusion. I grabbed her hips and pulled her backward, impaling her on my pipe. It felt like I was breaking into a wet, hot latex glove.

"Uhh!" She shuddered and began to bounce back and forth on me. "Smack my ass, daddy." She slammed backward harder and harder looking over her shoulder at me. She licked her juicy lips and moaned at the top of her lungs.

I smacked that big ass three times real hard. *Smack. Smack. Smack.* It jiggled along with her thick thighs. I shoved all ten hard inches into her and got to hitting that pussy like she owed me some money. I watched my pipe go in and out of her. Her lips would open to accommodate me, then close somewhat as I pulled back, only to open again. Thick traces of her gelatinous fluid leaked out of her vagina's mouth and slid down her thighs. The sight was overwhelming. On top of that, the Percocet had kicked in, heightening my sexual pleasure. I started to fuck her so fast and hard that my abs were hurting.

She closed her eyes and crashed back into me again and again. Her mouth hung wide open. She pulled up her tank top and released her B cup breasts that shook on her chest. Both nipples were heavily erect. *Whap! Whap!* I delivered two more smacks to her ass, causing her to yelp before she shuddered and came all over me.

I don't know how it happened, but less than a minute later, she was pushed into a ball with her knees to her chest with me ramming her hot pussy like a maniac. She rubbed all over my stomach muscles and scratched at my bulging chest. Then she pulled me down, so she could suck all over my lips. We breathed heavily into each other's faces while I continued to long-stroke her with a vengeance. No matter how hard I tried, or how long we stayed on that floor fucking like wild animals, the Percocet would not let me cum. It was frustrating because more than a few times I was right on the brink of the ultimate euphoria but could not make it over the edge.

After we showered and washed each other's body down from head to toe, I carried Kalani into my bedroom and laid her on the bed. She climbed across it and got under the covers naked. She held her arms wide open for me to join her. "Come on, bae. I need you to hold me for a minute. You already know how I get after you put that big ass dick on my lil' ass."

I laid down next to her and allowed for her to lay her head on my chest.

She rubbed up and down my stomach muscles, kissing them occasionally. "I just love the way you smell, Tristian. I always have. Did you know that?" She sniffed along my pubic hairs and kissed the head of my piece.

I laughed. "Shorty, don't think I don't see how yo' lil' ass done slipped into my bed again. What you think this make you; my woman or something?" I joked with her.

She raised her head and arched a brow. "We ain't about to get on that again, Tristian. Let's just enjoy the night and allow for me to comfort you during these tough times. I know you'd do the same for me." She shook her head and slid out of the bed with an attitude. She picked her tank top up from the floor and slid it over her head.

"What you doing?" I asked, looking up at her.

She started to mumble under her breath as she slid her panties up her thighs and sucked her teeth in disgust. "Every time shit is going good, you always gotta remind me of what it is between us. Damn, you be acting like I forgot or something." She sat on the edge of the bed and slid a sock onto her left foot.

I sat behind her naked and wrapped my arm around her shoulder. "What have I told you? I wanna hear you say it."

She sighed and her shoulders slumped inward. "Really? Do we gotta go through this right now?

Can't I just grab my car keys and get up with you tomorrow or something?"

I shook my head. "Nah, I wanna hear it."

She sighed. "You said that once I get my realtors license and my Bachelor of Science degree along with you, that we can begin to spend nights together. That in order for our relationship to be as strong as it needs to be, that there must be success on both ends. That you believe in me and need for me to believe in you just as much. We have to trust the process of hard work and allow for nothing to detour us, not even ourselves."

I kissed her cheek and then her neck. "That's all I'm saying. We gotta continue to earn each other, ma. It ain't a time to be playing house because we ain't got nothing to show for us just yet. But after this semester, once we get those degrees, then we can do our thing." I kissed her cheek again.

She stood up and looked down on me. "Do you really love me though, Tristian? Like fa real, fa real? The reason I ask is because I know hella bitches be jocking you and I'm always worried that before we accomplish our goals, one of them gon' snatch you away from me. I don't know how I'd handle that shit. I mean, I'm my own woman and everything, but I've invested way too much in your fine ass. I ain't going."

I pulled her on my lap and laughed. I kissed her neck and held her for a minute. "Kalani, you been a part of my life ever since I was a kid with no set goals or ambition. We've been through a lot together. I love you with everything that I am as a man. I only want the best for you because it's what you deserve one hundred percent. If a man doesn't motivate you to be the best version of yourself, then he is poison, not only to you but to himself as well. I know what you're capable of being, so I'ma motivate you until you achieve exactly that. I can't see myself ever settling for less or allowing somebody to steal your proven slot. That ain't the kid, and you know it. I'ma hold you down until we handle our business and make it happen for ourselves, together and individually."

She kissed my lips and rubbed my right ear. She had a habit of doing that whenever we were in close proximity. "Well, thank you, bae. You've been more of a man to me than my own father. I appreciate you more than you know, and I'll always be your rider until my last breath. Know that." She turned around and straddled me, laying her face in the crux of my neck.

Chapter 4

The next morning, I got up and made it to my old man's crib by ten o'clock. He stayed in a gated community in Bayclub Drive, New York, right off Riverton Square. It was always a process just to get past the gate keeper. Even though they knew I was his son, my Range Rover Sport was always searched from top to bottom along with myself. By the time I made it to my Pops' doorstep, I was irritated and ready to snap.

His maids had prepared a nice brunch for myself, my father, Showbiz, and Showbiz's full brother Miguel. Miguel was a nineteen-year-old pretty boy. He had a low cut and waves like myself, light brown eyes, and a teardrop under his right eye. He was born and raised in Havana, Cuba, but after getting into a war with a rival gang down that way, my father had brought him back to the States with him at the age of seventeen. He gave him a few blocks in Spanish Harlem where he could push his cocaine, and Miguel had been doing well ever since. He and I really didn't see eye to eye. I felt like he was jealous because of the relationship that me and Showbiz had, so we often butted heads. Since he'd moved to the States I'd already whooped his ass twice, and I honestly enjoyed it.

I dug into the plate of French toast, scrambled cheese eggs, sausage, a bowl of grits, and a tall glass of fresh squeezed orange juice. Across the table from me was my father. He was talking on two phones at once with a laptop on his lap. Miguel had an ear piece in his ear, talking while eating his brunch. He looked over to me a few times and curled his upper lip before looking off. I guess he thought he was looking hard or something. I didn't know. All it told me was that it was still bad blood between us and I needed to watch him. The first two ass whoopins had been because of his slick mouth. He had a habit of calling Black people niggers whenever he got mad at them. I wasn't having that shit. I checked his ass whenever I heard it, and that often led to me putting my foot up his ass, figuratively of course.

Showbiz didn't arrive at our father's house until about an hour after I had. He walked into the door with a bottle of Moet in his hand, sipping from it. He flopped down in the chair, and the maid filled his plate with food.

My father's mansion was always nice and clean. He had maids that worked on it around the clock. The inside was rich with Cuban culture from paintings of Fidel Castro to images of the island, and the ancestors of ours. From there he had a fifteen-meter swimming pool in the backyard, along with a tennis court. Crystal Chandeliers decorated the ceiling. The floors were marble. He had two sets of elevators inside of it. And everywhere you looked there was an armed Cuban guard pacing on high alert.

After we ate our meals, we wound up in the cinema room. We sat on the couches while my father stood in front of the dimly lit air-conditioned room with a black wife beater on over Gucci shorts and house shoes. He waved for Shapiro to step into the room before he began his talks.

"Okay, now that it appears that everyone is present, allow for me to proceed with the reason I've called you all here on this beautiful day. I'll be as brief as possible because time is money. I'll start with the announcement regarding Senator Jefferey Grant. I have decided to stand behind him in his pursuit to become the mayor of New York City. With my money and my influence, I am sure that I can make this happen. If it does, we'll all be very rich men. Not only us, but our family as a whole. If your father can conquer the city of New York, then we as Vegas can conquer the world. Trust me on this. There is only one problem." He sighed and lowered his head.

I frowned and adjusted myself on the couch. It seemed that my father's face turned a shade of white. I knew that whatever he was about to say was going to be earth shattering.

He ran his hand over his face and then his fingers through his hair. "Sons, I have a very progressive cancer in my pancreas. The doctors have told me that with surgery I'd be lucky if I lived two years more. Without it, I'm looking at eighteen months. Either way, things are looking dim for your father. But it has nothing to do with the success of our family. You three are the seeds of me. One of you will take over my position as head of this family when I am gone."

Showbiz stood up and shook his head. "Nah, I'm the oldest. If anybody is set to sit on that throne, it's me. By blood and rule I am next in line for the throne. You've been telling me this ever since I was a little boy." He snapped.

My eyes were still bugged out of my head. I couldn't believe that my father was dying. My old man. I couldn't imagine what life would be like without him. My throat was full of lumps. I felt like I was getting ready to break down to my knees. I just wanted to hug him. We could talk about everything else afterward. Suddenly, I needed a Percocet. I needed to feel numb. I slowly slid my hand into my pocket before popping one of the loose pills into my mouth, crushing it with my teeth. I felt the drug cascading down my throat, and it gave me an instant dose of euphoria.

"Sit down, Juanito!" My father snapped, calling my brother by his real name. He took a step toward him.

Showbiz flopped on the couch and mugged our father. "Explain to me why your seat is up for grabs, and why I won't inherit it like I'm supposed to." Showbiz said.

My eyes were stinging. I was watching my father closely now. He started to look skinnier to me. Fragile, and discolored. I stood up. "Yo, Pop, when did you first find out about this cancer, man? I can't see life without you in it." I stepped up to him and hugged him. I felt as sick as a dog.

"A month ago, Mijo, and don't worry. We'll discuss that further a little later. Thank you for being concerned about my well-being instead of my seat with this family." He shot daggers at Showbiz as I took my place back on the couch. "As far as you go. Shapiro, cut the lights."

Shapiro stood up and followed my father's command. As soon as the Cinema room was darkened, the projector was turned on.

The first thing I saw was Showbiz's red Porsche pulling into the parking lot of Holcombe Rucker Park. Then the camera zoomed in on Flex and his crew. Flex was bent over shining his rims with a rag. Showbiz pulled into a parking spot directly across from their trucks. You could see him and I exchanging dialogue before he jumped out of the Porsche and walked over to Flex with his arms outstretched at his sides.

My father paused the video. "This is a sign of negligence, arrogance, and stupidity. Not only were you outnumbered and in an area where we do not have the street's leverage, but you had my grandson with you when you took it upon yourself to become an idiot!"

Showbiz scrunched his face. "Pop, this nigga been owing me for way too long. I'd not been able to locate him ever since I'd given him the product. Was I not supposed to holler at him after I finally caught up to him?"

"Silence, Juanito!" He pushed the button on the remote so that the video played on.

It showed me in the Porsche looking over my shoulder at them. Then I looked out to the basketball courts. Maine shifted around in the backseat as if trying to get comfortable. The men around Flex backed away from Showbiz and him. Showbiz was nose to nose with Flex.

I got out of the Porsche and walked up to the basketball court. You could see me waving my arms for the kids to leave there. The little boys ignored me, waved me off and kept playing basketball. Across the way, Brittany, who'd been in the center of the double Dutch, jumped out of it. The other girls dropped the rope and began to run toward the exit of the courts.

The camera zoomed in on Showbiz as he slammed his gun under Flex's throat and flung him to the ground. They remained that way briefly. The little boys had run to the fence to see the fight better. Showbiz got up and walked to his Porsche with his back turned to Flex. Flex made his way from the ground, rushed to the front of the trucks and came up with what I'd once thought were .9 millimeters from a distance, but as the camera zoomed in on them I saw that they were nickel plated, ten-shot .45s. He cocked them and began to shoot, hitting Showbiz in the back, knocking him into the Porsche.

You saw the fire coming from my gun as I attempted to detour him from killing my brother. It appeared that my bullets shattered his headlights. He returned fire in my direction, along with his shooter. His shooter was bussing a Tech. That's when Brittany made a run for it. She got less than ten feet away from me when she fell face-first into the concrete, shaking on the pavement. I saw Showbiz shooting over the back of his Porsche. His bullets struck the windshield of one of the trucks. It shattered. Showbiz pulled Maine over the car and to him. I saw me running across the playground, so I could cover the defenseless Brittany. I jerked twice in the air before falling on top of her where I covered her protectively. Flex jumped in one of the trucks and pulled in front along the side of the Porsche. The back door opened, and more shots were fired. Showbiz ducked, waiting for the shooting to stop, then popped his head up. He aimed at the truck, but no fire came from his gun. I surmised that it had jammed. The next thing he did was unthinkable.

"Pops turn that shit off, man. We don't need to be seeing this," he snapped.

"Sit your ass down, Mijo. Now!" My father hollered, pausing the video. "If you were man enough to do what you've done, then you're man enough to accept your brother's opinions of your actions. Now, sit!"

Showbiz made a move for the door when two of my father's Cuban bodyguards blocked his path. He looked them up and down, then plopped down on the couch in defeat.

The video began again. It showed the back door of the truck opening. Showbiz jumped up, ducked and made a run for it. As soon as he did, Maine jumped up to follow him. The camera zoomed in on Flex smiling. He bit into his lower lip, aimed, and pulled the trigger twice, blowing half of Maine's face off. My nephew's neck jerked twice before he fell on his face. A puddle of blood formed around him. The two trucks stormed out of the parking lot. Showbiz was hiding behind a big, blue metal dumpster until they sped away. Only then did he run back over to check on Maine.

My father shut the television off and glared at him with mounting anger. "Explain yourself."

Showbiz swallowed and lowered his head. "I don't know what I was thinking, Pops, honestly. All I knew was that my gun had jammed. I had to get out of there before they wasted me. I'd already caught four to my vest. I mean, I didn't know that Maine was going to jump and follow behind me. I—"

My father turned his back on him. "You think that I'm going to put some ignorant, impulsive, two-bit street hustler on the throne of this family when I've spent the last thirty years getting us to the status that we are now?" He scoffed. "You're out of your fucking mind." He turned around and looked me in the eyes. "Nothing is given freely that a man will cherish. A real man will only respect and honor the things in this life that are earned through blood sweat, tears, and strategy. I have no more than a year left on my life. Before I leave this earth, I will choose one of you to become King of Vegas."

Showbiz shook his head. "So, you gon' take my birthright? All because I made a mistake?" He frowned. "I'm not perfect, Pop. Ain't no man walking this earth is."

"In order to be king, you must be, Mijo. Not only does this video show your imperfections, but it shows your utter lack of intelligence. You could have been the cause of four lives being lost. Not once have you apologized for the position you placed your brother in. I believe it's honestly because you don't care about anybody other than yourself, Juanito. Your heart seems to be as cold as the bandits of Havana."

I didn't need for Showbiz to apologize to me. I knew what I was getting into by having him pick me up from the airport. He never failed to get into some bull crap. It was just the man he was.

Showbiz lowered his head and remained silent. He picked up the bottle of Moet and chugged it down.

My father rolled his head around on his neck and exhaled loudly. "In order to put Jefferey Wagner in office, I need to contribute no less than fifteen million dollars to his campaign over the next five months. That's a minimum of three million dollars a month. The only dilemma is that I have business interests all over New York. I am tied up. It's just the way the game goes. However, I have three sons that are in contention for this throne. Once Grant is in office it will catapult us to levels that are beyond belief. New York is the epicenter and nucleus of the world. The man sitting on this throne has to know how to network and conquer those that are sitting in seats slightly above him."

Shapiro turned on the projector and shut the light back off.

My father clicked a controller in his hand, and a picture of The Red Hook Housing Projects that I'd grown up in came across the screen. "This is the Red Hook Houses. They are the cocaine capital of America. They are run by the Gomez family who are bitter enemies from Havana. Bruno Gomez had just been indicted and apprehended by the DEA while vacationing in Hawaii only a month ago. Since he's been off the scene, his twins have taken over the operations. They are calling themselves the Gomez Kings. More than one hundred of the Latin Kings from Havana have joined forces with these two, and they are slowly cornering the cocaine market. The Red Hook Houses make a million dollars a day during the weekdays, and two million on weekends. These houses need to become the Vegas. Wisin and Chulo must be handled in a such a way that it sends a message to the underworld that the Vegas aren't to be messed with." He nodded and looked each of us in the eyes yet ended with his pinned on me. "Tristian, you grew up in these houses. You know them in and out. That's why on this operation I'm making you my lead to see what you do. I trust that you will draw up a well calculated plan before anything is executed. If you can conquer these houses and bring fifteen million dollars to me before the five-month deadline, this throne is yours. That doesn't mean that you neglect your studies the slightest. I look forward to attending your graduation at the end of this semester. Understand me?"

I nodded and bowed my head to him out of respect and admiration. "I can handle it, Pop. I won't let you down." Even though I was saying that out of my mouth, I was scared out of my mind that I was going to let him down. I mean, the Red Hook Houses were serious. Four of five people got murdered in there every single day. The police rarely ever made an appearance, and even when they did they had to be given permission from some of the bosses that oversaw the buildings. I grew up fighting every single day when I was young there. I'd lost more than a few close homies that were my age to the gun before I was even ten years old. To accomplish the mission my Pops was setting before me, I had to think outside of the box. I knew that I could do it. I was underestimating myself.

Showbiz jumped up and sucked his teeth. "Hell n'all! You finna put this task in his lap just because he going to college? What type of shit is that, Pop? I'm in them streets every single day. I don't fear Wisin or Chulo. I was ready to go at they old man before the feds got him, but you told me to chill. Remember that?"

"And why do you think it was that I told you to chill, Mijo? If you can tell me that then this mission will be all your own. Your brother will continue in college, and I will leave the streets to you. Tell me."

Showbiz scrunched his eyebrows. He crossed his arms and held his chin in his right hand in deep thought.

I knew the answer off the back, but I just wanted to see if my brother had enough common sense to know it as well. I never liked beefing with him because whenever we went at each other, we went all out. Some of our fights against each other had been the worst.

Showbiz lowered his arms and smiled. "You didn't want us to start a big war with another family because it would have been bad for business, right?"

"And you, Miguel. Why do you think I asked him to refrain from going at Bruno Gomez? Keep in mind that your brother couldn't be more wrong at this juncture."

"What?" Showbiz waved him off and plopped back on the couch.

"Is it because it would affect the businesses back in Havana? I know that you've recently bought a hundred acres of their sugarcane fields. Maybe it was too early to start a beef with them."

My father shook his head. "While that's thought out and feasible, you're wrong. What about you, Tristian? Why do you think I didn't allow for your brother to proceed with war against the Gomez's?"

"It's because you had inside information that Mr. Bruno Gomez was being tracked by the Federal Government. If they were watching his every move and keeping him under heavy surveillance, and you had allowed for Showbiz to attack him, there was a great chance that he would have been caught in the act, and thus bringing intense heat down onto our family. In the Federal Government's eyes, it would have been killing two birds with one stone." I knew my father played the political game better than anybody in New York city. He kept tabs on everybody who he felt was important or a potential enemy. He'd told me and Showbiz this time and time again. He'd say to conquer the game you must know the players inside and out. The only movies a true King Pin should watch are the ones that feature his enemies and the competition. I watched my father very closely because I looked up to him. He was a true Don in my opinion.

He walked over and placed his hand on my shoulder. "To be aware is to conquer all, Mijo. Which is why it's important for our family to get Senator Grant into his Mayoral position. From there the sky is the limit for the Vegas."

"Wait, so he was right?" Showbiz asked, looking up to my father.

My pops nodded. "I tell you all the time that you must know your enemy inside and out. Not only your enemy but those that are playing the same game that you are because, at the end of the day, there can only be one King. New York is a Pride, and in this Pride, we are all lions, but there can only be one true King. I am certain that this King is in this room. That King is a Vega." He squeezed my shoulder and walked back to the projector. "The goal is fifteen million in five months. That's three million a month. Whichever one of my sons are able to set this amount in front of me before the deadline, you are the one that will inherit my seat and all the power that comes along with it."

I was confused. "So, Pops, are you saying that the money is the most important thing, or is conquering the Red Hook Houses the most important? Where do the Gomez's fit into all of this?"

He wagged his finger at me and smiled. "Your questions are always the right ones, Mijo." He shook his head.

Showbiz flared his nostrils and clenched his teeth.

My father peeped it. They made eye contact. "You're free to ask as many questions as you want as well, Juanito. There is no reason to sit on the sidelines if there is something on your mind."

Showbiz looked off, huffing and puffing. I could tell that he was upset, but I didn't care. I needed to know where my pops was going with things.

"The Red Hook Houses represent generational wealth if we can take them over and away from the Gomez's. The Gomez's are using the money that they make from the housing projects to fund and strengthen their operations back in Havana. They are buying up acres of land, turning them into poppy fields and Cocoa plants. At the same time, they can strengthen their regime back home. All Cuba understands is money. It's all they respect. The Gomez's are setting themselves in a position to sit beside the Castro's. Once this happens, our family's bloodline becomes in jeopardy because we are the next strongest family in Cuba. The Gomez's will be looking to wipe us out. We must cut them off at the source. The source is the Red Hook Houses."

I nodded and understood what he was saying one hundred percent. We had to pounce on the Gomez's before they became too powerful and turned us into the enemy. The one who controlled the money controlled not only their portions of America, but our homeland.

Showbiz wiped his mouth with his hand. "A'ight then, I see what it is. But I feel like if you gon' allow for one of us to come through with the fifteen million in five months' time, you should also see which son will be able to conquer these Projects before that same deadline. I'm more than up for the task." He looked over at me and smiled.

I nodded. "Yeah, Pop, let's do it like that. The goal is fifteen million and the Red Hook Houses. The son that can set both before your feet in five months' time should be groomed and able to inherit your throne, along with all of the political connections that will come into fruition with the election of Jefferey Grant into office."

My father ran his fingers through his hair and sighed. He looked from me to Showbiz, then down to Miguel. "Okay. But listen to me. Just because this is a competition does not mean that I am not here for each one of you. I will guide, direct, and give you sound advice for you to adhere to. At the end of the day we are family, and it's all about the advancement of our family. I love all three of you, and I wish you all the best. Juanito, you stay behind. We need to talk about the footage that we've just gone over, and what your punishment will be."

Chapter 5

Shapiro told me that Brittany was finally out of the Intensive Care Unit on a Thursday, a month after the shooting had taken place. Shapiro told me that the main nurse that was in charge of her was able to keep tabs on her for him. She'd said that Brittany's eyes were finally opened, and she was awake and speaking. They were not able to remove the bullet from her spine without it causing some major damage. As it stood, she had been told that she was paralyzed from the waist down. That she would never walk again. I was devastated and just had to see her no matter how much Shapiro advised strongly against it.

I showed up at the hospital one early Friday morning with a bouquet of white roses in my hands, a diamond Tennis bracelet from Tiffany's, and so many Get Well Soon balloons that I should have floated away into the sky it seemed. I just wanted to make a great impression on her. I didn't know what exactly I was going to say to her, but I felt the need to be in her presence. The nurse had assured Shapiro that I would be able to speak with her for at least ten minutes. She said she'd somehow manage it. I didn't know how, and I didn't ask. I just wanted to see her.

When I got inside of the hospital, the short Arab young woman guided me through the hospital and up to Brittany's room. The nurse was about 5'3". She had blue eyes and bronzed skin. She also had a very large nose and a hijab over her head. She turned to me in the elevator as we made our way up to Brittany's floor. "Listen to me, Mr. Vega, you literally only have ten minutes before her mother shows up.

She's given me permission to watch over her child while she works a few hours throughout the night at the women's shelter down the road. She was just going down to feed them breakfast this morning and due to return at about nine o'clock. If she comes back and sees you in the room she's probably going to freak out. Do we understand each other?"

I nodded and smiled. I felt as if I was going on a date for the first time in my life. I was so excited to see Brittany that I didn't know what to do. "Thank you for this opportunity. I'll do my best to honor your time structure."

* * *

The nurse helped Brittany to sit up in the bed. She looked drowsy. Her lips were white, and from the last time I'd seen her in the park, she looked as if she'd lost about ten pounds. "Brittany, we have somebody that's here to see you. Can you sit up for a minute?" She asked her.

Brittany winced and squeezed her eyelids tight together. "Where is my mother?" She asked.

There were IVs in her arms. Beside her was a machine that beeped every second. The room was all white and smelled of rubbing alcohol. There was a small couch in the corner of it, right next to an open bathroom door.

The nurse situated her pillow up under her. "She stepped out for a second to feed the homeless women down the road. She'll be back very soon. In the meantime, allow me to introduce you to Mr. Vega. He was present when all of this took place."

Brittany smacked her lips and turned her head, so she was facing me. "I remember you. You were the man that told all of us kids to get out of the park before those men started shooting. Those boys didn't listen, but I was trying to." Her voice sounded dry and raspy.

I rushed to her bedside and handed her the bouquet of white roses. "These are for you, lil' mama. I'm so sorry that all of this happened to you. I wish I could take this pain away from you. You're a princess and you didn't deserve what happened."

She smiled weakly. "Thank you. The doctors say that I ain't ever gon' walk again, but I don't believe them. I don't want to stay in a bed for the rest of my life. I want to run track like Allison Felix. She's my hero. I'm gon' be just like her when I grow up."

I took a deep breath and felt the lump form in my throat. I couldn't help from brushing her bangs from her forehead. She was so beautiful. So precious. Her eyes were light brown just like mine. "Don't listen to those doctors. You'll walk again. I believe in you. I'm going to be right by your side when you take that first step." I opened the box from Tiffany's and took out the diamond tennis bracelet. Took her right wrist and fastened it around it. "I bought this for you just to say that I am with you, and I will be every step of the way. I'm sorry about what happened."

She brought the bracelet up to her eyes and looked it over. "Wow, this is beautiful. Are you sure that you bought it for me?" She smiled.

I nodded. "I'll get you anything that you want. You're a princess. I mean that."

She opened her arms and I felt like my heart skipped a couple beats. "I have to give you a hug, Mr. Vega. Not just for this stuff, but you were on top of me when the bullets started to pop everywhere. You're my hero too."

I stepped into her arms and hugged her, laying her head on my chest. I held her with tears streaming down my cheeks. "With physical therapy, we will do all that we can. I only need for you to be strong, and to fight. I'll take care of everything else. I want you to keep this card close by your side. If you need anything, you call me. I don't care what it is. Do you understand that, lil' mama?"

She took the card and put it under her fluffy pillow. "Yes."

I kissed her on the forehead again and rubbed her cheek. "I'm sorry once again."

She smiled. "Mr. Vega, can I ask you a question?"

"Sure! Baby, you can ask me anything." I kneeled beside her.

"Was my uncle shooting at you or that other car?"

I was confused. "Your uncle? Who is your uncle, princess?"

She furrowed her eyebrows. "Flex. He's my mother's little brother. I think he was mad, that's why he and his friends started shooting."

I looked over to the nurse. She shrugged before tapping her watch. She looked out of the door, into the hallway more than once.

I stood up and kissed the back of Brittany's hand. "I don't think he was shooting at me, but I did get hit.

Me and your uncle have never had problems before. But don't you worry about that. You focus on getting healthy. In the meantime, anything that you need, you make sure you don't hesitate to call me."

* * *

I sat on the edge of my bed with head lowered, trying to think everything over. I was finally able to connect the dots about Flex and Perjah's relationship. I wondered if Brittany had told her that Flex had been one of the shooters. I wondered how involved he was in Brittany's life, and what would allow for him to start shooting while she was in the vicinity. It seemed careless if you asked me. Just as careless as what Showbiz had done with regards to Maine.

The wounds in my back began to throb. I jumped out of the bed and grabbed two Percocet thirties, and swallowed them, chasing them with a handful of water. I was longing for the high. I needed to feel numb once again.

Later that night, Kalani buzzed my doorbell. I opened the door to find her dressed in a tight Eves St. Laurent dress that stopped just below her crotch. She had a bottle of Ace of Spades in her hand and a big smile on her face. "Baby, I want you to come out with me tonight." She stepped forward and kissed my lips.

I hugged her, looking down and into her brown eyes. "You popping bottles and shit. What's the occasion?" I asked, gripping that fat booty and kissing her neck.

She sucked her teeth. "Damn, it gotta be a special occasion for me to go out and spend some time with you now?" She took a step   back and placed her right hand on her hip.

"N'all, baby, it ain't nothing like that. I just got a lot on my mind. There's a whole bunch of things that I gotta figure out in a short amount of time. You know how I get when I'm contemplating."

She stomped her left foot on the porch. "I know, baby, but I want to go out. Damn." She sighed. "Okay then. If you must know, Shirley Colfax, the number one realtor, and owner of the richest real estate company in the state of New York has offered me a job the second I receive my license. Do you know what that means? It means that I'll be at the number one company in the state. I'll have a salary of a hundred thousand dollars a year. She says that I'll make ten percent from each sale. Majority of her properties are out in the Hamptons and upper Manhattan. We're talking some serious cash, Tristian, and all I want to do is share this moment with you before I take that exam next week. Is that so wrong?" She sucked on her bottom lip and looked into my eyes all sexy like.

I grabbed her to me and kissed those juicy lips. "Shirley Colfax, huh? I guess you call yourself falling   your dreams then?" I smiled with our noses pressed   against one another's. Then I slid my tongue into her mouth, sucking all over her lips.

* * *

It was a nice, breezy night, about seventy or so degrees in the city of New York. Kalani sat across the table from me at Davino's Italian restaurant in Brooklyn. Davino's was a nice four-star restaurant where most of the dope boys out of Brooklyn dined whenever they wanted to chill and talk business or take their woman out to a lovely place that wasn't too far away from the borough. The menu was high priced. The service was top-notch. The atmosphere was soothing and calm. Davion's had a four-piece orchestra that played on a stage in the center of the restaurant. The tables and booths were situated strategically around it. They were nicely spaced from one another, and the dim lights allowed for each patron's privacy. Me and Kalani had been here a few times. It was sorta like our spot.

I reached across the table and brushed her curly hair out of her face and tucked it behind her left earlobe. She was beautiful. It seemed like the older we got the finer she became to me. I'd only had a few dreams where I saw myself walking down the aisle of a church in preparation to be married. Each time I got to the front of the church in those dreams, I always saw her being there as my bride. I loved and cared about her a great deal. After we accomplished our individual goals I saw myself putting that ring on her finger. That was a little ways down the road, but I saw it.

"Baby, you look beautiful tonight. I like how you whipped your lil' curls so that they fell over your shoulders like this. You did ya' thing, ma."

She smiled and batted her long eyelashes at me. "Thank you, baby. I do what I can for you. I'm glad that you noticed."

I rubbed the side of her cheek and looked into her pretty brown eyes. "You know you gon' pass that test with flying colors, right? You ain't about to let nothing stand in your way. Ain't that right?"

She shook her head. "Nothing, or no one. One of the only ways for a woman to exert her dominance on this world is to become successful in her own right. My success will level the playing field in this dog-eat-dog world. Statistically the odds are against me because of where I come from, but for me it's motivation." She took her knife and fork, cutting a piece of the lasagna and forking it up into her mouth. She chewed with her eyes closed. "Mmm, they still got it."

I scanned the restaurant with Brittany on my brain. I was praying that she was okay. Ever since I'd left the hospital she'd been my every other thought. I felt a deep connection with her.

"What about you, baby? Are you prepared for this semester? I mean like mentally prepared? You seem like you're struggling with something that's getting the best of you. Care to talk about it?"

"I was just thinking about the little girl that got hit up at the park a lil' while back. I went over and saw her today. She was bright and smiling. They say she's paralyzed from the waist down and that she may never walk again."

Kalani leaned over the table and placed her hand on top of mine. "Aw, baby, that's sad. But it's not your fault. You did everything that you could to save her. I'm pretty sure she knows that. So, what's eating at you?"

"It turns out that one of the shooters was her uncle. The nigga Flex that Showbiz was getting at is her kin. When I found that out today it blew my wig back."

Kalani sighed. "So, what's going through your mind?"

"You know how my brother get down. Whenever somebody wrongs him, he likes to take it out on their whole family. Since he lost Maine, I can see him finding out about Brittany being kin to Flex and using it against her. My brother always been cold like that."

Kalani shrugged. "I mean, you already know how it is where we come from. War is war. Showbiz been getting down like this ever since I've known him. Why are you so stressed over him doing him? You lost a whole ass nephew. That should be your concern, not this little girl."

I felt my temper rising. "You see what I'm saying? That is the same logic that got one child in the grave and the other in the hospital paralyzed from the waist down. It shouldn't be like that. If I'm going to kill a nigga, then all my bullets should go into him, not some baby. I can't with that shit, and I almost slapped the fuck out of you because I expect for you to have more common sense than that."

She snatched her hand away and mugged me. "Really? Over some fucking kid that you don't even know?" She rolled her eyes. "How many people from her side have checked in to make sure that you're okay? After all, you took two bullets to your back as well. What if those bullets would have hit your spine and you were paralyzed for the rest of your life? Then what?"

"Then I'd a took that shit like a man because I am a man. Those are kids. They shouldn't have to be forced to endure those consequences. They were at a park being babies. Because of these dumb ass niggas their lives were changed forever. That's fucked up." I pushed my plate of Fettuccini Alfredo away from me and tossed the huge napkin from my lap into the plate.

Kalani shook her head. "I love you and all, Tristian, but you have too much of a fucking conscious. You're sitting here fucking up our evening because of something your brother did. Something that you tried to prevent. It makes absolutely no sense to me. Can we please focus in on me? Remember my whole Shirley Colfax news?"

I looked into her eyes, then over her shoulder as Wisin Gomez stepped into the restaurant with his arm around a well-known video vixen by the name of Sevyn. He had a white Cocoa Cola quarter length mink on his back, Gucci pants and Balenciaga shoes on his feet. He was full blooded Cuban. His hair was shaved at the sides and into a short, curly mohawk. He had gold ropes around his neck, and white diamonds in his earlobes. Behind him were two bodyguards that looked as if they were from the islands.

I eyed him closely, and because I was, Kalani looked over her shoulder at him. "Mmm, there go Wisin's fine ass, and he's with that bum ass bitch Sevyn. Ugh."

That was one of the things about Kalani. On one hand she was one of those females that I saw myself being with for a long time. But then on the other hand, she was so ghetto and even a bit immature. The fact the she was so damn intelligent was often lost because of her unconscious outbursts that happened often at the wrong time. What type of man wanted to be on a date with his woman and hear her call another dude fine? That shit was irritating.

I grabbed a handful of her hair and yanked her shit so hard that her cheek went into the lasagna. "Bitch, you wanna go over there and sit with that nigga and tell his bitch to come fuck with me? Huh?" I growled into her face.

"Let me go, Tristian. Damn. I ain't mean it like that." She tried to pry my fingers loose from her hair.

"Every time you do something right, you always fuck something up in the next breath. That shit get old." I let go of her hair and pushed her face backward, muffing her ass.

She stood up and scooted her chair back loudly. "Don't be grabbing my muthafucking hair like that. What the fuck is wrong with you?" She screamed at me.

"Bitch, you better sit yo' ass down and quit making a scene."

"Fuck you, Tristian. Fuck you and that lil' girl that got you all bent and out of shape. It ain't your fuckin' problem!"

Wisin looked over in our direction with his arm tightly around Sevyn's shoulder. He had a big smile on his face.

Our maître d came over with his hands raised chest high. "I'm sorry, but if there's a problem, I'm going to have to ask you to leave."

Kalani grabbed her Birkin bag off the chair and pushed it up to the table, then chucked her plate of food to the floor. "I'm tire of this shit!" she hollered.

I stood up and dropped two one hundred-dollar bills on the table. On the way to the door, me and Wisin made eye contact. He smiled at me and shook his head. I couldn't wait to really give him a reason to shake it. The expression "Laugh now, cry later," came into mind.

When we got outside, Kalani was against the car with her arms crossed over her chest. I unlocked the doors and we got into my Range Rover. She slammed the door and almost yanked the seatbelt out of the socket.

"Shorty, you better chill yo' ass out, I know that."

"I ain't better do a muthafucking thing but stay Black and die. Keep your punk ass hands to yourself. I ain't your bitch just yet. You made that perfectly clear, remember?"

I started the truck and was about to pull out of my parking space when my phone buzzed. I looked at the face and didn't recognize the number. A text came across the screen that read, "This Perjah. We need to talk, ASAP." She ended it with an angry faced emoji.

Kalani looked at me. "Who is that? One of your lil' hoes?"

I shook my head. "N'all. This is Perjah; the lil' girl's mother. She say we need to talk."

She rolled her eyes. "Just drop me off before you get to doing all that shit. Had I known the evening was gon' go like this, I would've celebrated with someone else. Thanks for nothing." She slammed her back against the seat and let the window down a lil' bit.

We made it back to my brownstone. We'd ridden the whole way in silence. When I pulled behind her black Mazda, before I could apologize to her for what had taken place at Davion's, she jumped out of the truck and slammed the door. "You make me sick, Tristian. All I asked you for was one good night. You couldn't even give me that. Well, fuck you! I don't need for you to be there for me anymore!" She opened the door of her car, got in and sped away from the curb which sent smoke from the tires wafting into the air.

I sat there for a long time wondering if I had been in the wrong for doing what I'd done to her. I loved that girl like crazy. It was just that sometimes she got the best of my emotions and brought that animal out of me. The animal that I tried my best to keep dormant.

Chapter 6

A week after Perjah had hit my phone saying that we needed to talk, she had finally agreed to us having a sit down in the cafeteria at Mount Sinai hospital while the Arab nurse gave Brittany a sponge bath. I'd been bussing my ass in my studies, trying to obtain that Bachelor of Science degree, simultaneously the ordeal with my father and brothers weighed heavily on my mind and conscious. I knew that I had a lot to figure out and planned on doing so real soon.

When I walked into the cafeteria, Perjah stood up and extended her hand. She was dressed in a smock that read *The Harbor House* across the front of it. I figured that she'd just gotten off work or was on her way to work at the women's shelter down the road from the hospital. Either way, I was happy that she'd agreed to meet with me.

I shook her hand. "Thank you for meeting with me, Perjah. Honestly, it means a lot."

"Yeah, well I don't know if you're going to feel the same way after we talk." She walked around the table and sat down. "Please have a seat."

I sat. The cafeteria only had a few other people that were there. I saw two nurses sitting side by side one another, chatting about something or the other. Behind them were two older women eating grilled cheese sandwiches, and tomato soup.

"Mr. Vega, I don't appreciate you going behind my back and visiting with my daughter without my permission. She dug into pocket and placed the diamond bracelet I'd given Brittany on the table,

73

pushing it across to me. She's not allowed to accept gifts from strangers."

I pushed it back across to her. "Perjah, I'm not a stranger. I just want to be a part of her recovery. I want to help you guys out in any way that I can. Don't deny me of this right. I am begging you."

"You have no rights to my daughter. Now I am asking you to stay away from her *and* I. We don't need anything from you, or your family. You got it?"

I looked into her penetrating eyes for a long time, then shook my head. "Why won't you allow me to do what's right? Don't you know that I would buss my ass to get her the best doctors and physical therapists in New York. And not just here. I'd fly them in if I had to. I just want to make things right, Perjah. That little girl deserves the best life possible."

She slammed her hand on the table. "That little girl belongs to me and her name is Brittany." She lowered her eyes. "Now I can understand that you're experiencing some form of guilt and it's making you feel some type of way, but we don't need your pity. My daughter is strong, and she will overcome this with me by her side, and nobody else. It's been us for a long time now, and we've never needed a savior. Take your diamond tennis bracelet and your guilty conscience and stay the fuck away from me and my little girl. This is your last warning." She stood up, pointed at me with her pinky finger. "I'm not kidding." Then she walked away, looking over her shoulder at me twice before disappearing.

I sat there for a long time lost in thought. I'd respected her gangsta, and how she was able to stand up to me like a mother bear. Fearless. Her brown eyes never left mine. I could tell that she wasn't intimidated by my size, or the fact of me being in the streets. She'd rejected a $5,000 bracelet as if it was nothing. I felt that she was a woman of principle. One that would not allow for anyone or anything to stand in the way of her beliefs, or her baby girl. I honored that, and as crazy as it was to admit, I'd become drawn to her after only one meeting. I had to find a way penetrate her rough exterior. She had some serious walls built up. I had to either break through or jump over them. Either way, I refused to keep my distance. I had to become a part of Brittany's life to make sure that she was always well taken care of. In my mind it was my responsibility to make sure that Brittany was good for the rest of her life. I knew that Showbiz didn't care about her.

As far as I could see, other than Flex, Perjah was handling things on her own. Doctor's bills were expensive. So were hospital stays. I didn't know where she worked, or what type of income she brought in, but I could only imagine that it wasn't enough to sustain what her and Brittany were going through.

I rose from the table and picked up my phone, dialing up Shapiro. I had to find out what type of bills Perjah was faced with. Then I would find a way to relieve her of those burdens.

* * *

Showbiz rolled up on me just as I was getting out of my truck later that night. He pulled alongside my driver's side and rolled down his passenger's window. "Tristian, jump in this bitch for a minute. Let me holler at you." He leaned across the console and pushed open the door his 2019 Benz truck.

My stomach was starting to cramp, and I had one of the worst headaches I'd ever had. I needed a few of those pills to be in my system. I was starting to jones for them. "Yo, give me a minute to run in the crib, Kid. I'll be right back out."

He nodded and pulled his truck into the open parking space in front of mine. As soon as he did, some chicks from the stoop next door walked up to his truck and began to flirt with him. They were your average run of the mill gold diggers that stalked niggas with hot cars and alleged back rolls. They were sisters, both caramel, and nosey as all out outdoors. Any gossip that was being spread through the hood it was probably because of them.

When I got inside of the crib, I double-timed to my bedroom and pulled the bottle of Percocet pills out of my top dresser drawer. The bottle felt light. I shook it and it sounded like there was only a few left. I began to panic. My stomach turned into knots. The wounds on my back started to scream louder than a victim being tortured to death. I opened the top and turned the bottle upside down. One lonely pill fell into my hand.

I was devastated. "Fuck!" One thirty wasn't about to do nothing for me. Sixties were barely scratching the surface. I knew I'd have to get a refill that night. *Hopefully I could find a twenty-four-hour CVS that would take my prescription* was the only thing that was going through my mind.

I took the one lonely pill and crushed it into dust on top of my dresser. I had to take this one to the head. The only way I felt I could really get the chance to feel it is if I snorted it, so that's what I did. I made two lines and sent one line up each nostril. The drug hit me harder than ever. I felt like my body was completely numb and floating on air.

When I climbed into Showbiz's Benz, he handed me an Uzi with a fifty-round clip hanging out of the handle. I took it and sat it over my lap. "What's this for?"

"I got the low down on where this fool Flex chilling at. I want you to roll out with me. We about to sweat this nigga and make him pay for his sins. Nah'mean?" Showbiz picked up a bottle of pink Sprite and turned it up, burping afterward.

I frowned. "What's good with you, bruh? You think killing this nigga about to make you feel better or what?"

"I'll determine all that after I put that nigga in a casket. Word is bond. I ain't been able to sleep ever since my lil' nigga got taken off this earth. Whether the family feel like it's my fault or not, I gotta make amends." He took another swallow from the Sprite, killing it, and tossed the empty bottle out of the window. "This fuck nigga over on West 154th and 7th Avenue, over in Harlem. I got one of my lil' bitches up under him. They having a lil' get together for this nigga birthday. Once we hit his ass up I'ma put one in her melon too. No harm, no foul. Bitch pussy getting old anyway." He wiped his nose and sniffed loudly.

"Bruh, are you sure that you got all of your ducks in a row? We ain't about to just pop up over here and freestyle shit, right? My brother had a habit of winging things. He was impulsive. It was one of his major downfalls.

"Yo', I been listenin' to Pops chew me out for the last few weeks because of what happened to my seed. I wish that drone would've crashed, and he would have never have gotten that footage. He been treatin' me like a bumpy ever since then. I can barely accept that from him. I definitely ain't about to take it from you." He mugged me with anger.

"Fuck how you feelin'. Nigga, I need to know that you got everything in place before we get there. I ain't trying to get burned by that steel ever again. At least not because of somebody else's fuck up. I'll burn anything over you; you know that shit. So, holler at me, Kid. Word up."

He reached inside his Gucci pocket and popped two Mollies. He crushed his with his teeth and swallowed them, then handed me one. "Here, take this Molly. Maybe it'll help yo' ass calm down a little bit. I need you to be on straight killer mode like you used to be when we were teens. Ever since you been going to college you done softened up a little bit. I ain't feeling that shit." He curled his lip and sucked his teeth loudly. "I got everything under control. By the end of the night this nigga, Flex, a be taking a dirt nap. I wanna empty my whole clip in his face, reload, and slump him all over again."

I exhaled slowly through my nose and closed my eyes. It never

Failed. Whenever I rotated with my brother, there was always some bullshit involved. And my first mind always told me to shake his ass, but I never listened. I think it was because I still looked up to him and loved all him with all my heart. I felt that if he made an unwise decision that could cost him his life this time, at least I'd be there to have his back and to save him from meeting the Reaper. Even though he was my older brother I felt the need to protect him against all odds. "Bruh, I'm down for whatever. I'ma buss this gun until ain't nothing left in the clip. I'm still a Vega."

He looked over at me and smile with lossy eyes. "That's what I'm talking about, lil' bruh. Bring that killa shit up out of you and let's handle this business. Let's do this shit for, Maine."

* * *

It was pitch black on the block that Flex held his birthday gathering on. All the streets lights had been shot out. It was hot and humid this night. So much so that my vest was itching my chest and sticking to me worse than ever. I could hear music coming out of one of upstairs windows as we made our way onto the stoop.

As soon as we got to the top stair, the door opened, and a Puerto Rican chick stepped out and ran up to Showbiz, wrapping her arms around him. "Ay, Papi. You took forever. Flex is upstairs right now with a stripper on his lap. She's giving him one of the best lap dances of his life. He's fucked up and out of his mind on Xanax and Percocet. Do whatever you wanna do, just don't harm my girl." She kissed him on the cheek and stepped back into the door way, wanting us to follow her.

I had a half of mask covering my face and so did Showbiz. I cocked the Uzi and made my way inside the brownstone right behind him and the Rican. We slowly made our way upstairs. The sounds of The Lox could be heard banging out of the speakers. The stairs creaked under our feet, but I doubted anyone heard them upstairs because of the music.

My stomach was doing somersaults. It did that every time I was put in a position to kill somebody. It would be easy to say that taking a life was easy, but for me it wasn't. I had a bit of a conscious. I never liked killing unless I absolutely had to. Because Flex had killed my nephew, I felt that fit the bill of being necessary. I couldn't live that down. I still remembered the smile on his face before he pulled the trigger. I saw it every time I closed my eyes at night. For that alone I had to take part on giving, Flex, ass the business.

When we got to the top of the stairs, the Rican chick stood with her back to the door and put her finger to her lips. "He gon' be to your right sitting on the couch. Remember, whatever you about to do, don't hit my girl. A'ight?" She looked from me to Showbiz.

Showbiz laughed and nodded. He pulled out a .9 millimeter with a silencer on the front of it from the small of his back. "Yeah, a'ight, bitch." He grabbed her by the throat, pressed the barrel of the gun to her forehead and pulled the trigger before throwing her lifeless body down the stairs.

I wiped her blood from my cheek and looked down at her with my eyes wide open. The whole situation had caught me off guard. "What the fuck, Kid?"

"Dead men can't tell no tales, bruh. Let's handle this business." He pulled open the door and stormed inside with me right behind him.

The lights were dimmed. The music was blaring so loud that I could barely hear myself think. The front door led into the living room. There was a long wooden table with a bunch of half-emptied liquor bottles, and a box of Garcia Vega cigars. The chairs around the table had coats on the back of them. There was a ceiling fan that appeared to be on high. It threatened to fall off the ceiling as it spun around and around.

I had the Uzi hung to my side, as I scanned house. Showbiz jogged to his right, with me right behind him. When we got to the front portion of the house, I saw three strippers dancing in front of Flex and two of his boys. The strippers had their hands on the floor, shaking their naked asses while Flex and his boys threw dollar bills at them and joked amongst themselves. One of Flex's men was just standing up to pour some of his champagne on one of the stripper's asses when he looked to his left and must've seen us approaching. He dropped the bottle and held his hands in the air.

Showbiz covered the distance quickly. He rushed him, and popped him twice in the face, knocking meat his taco. Then turned his gun to Flex's other guy and shot him once in the forehead. He fell over the couch on his chest with both of his legs kicking like crazy.

The strippers screamed and fell on their bottoms, scooting backward beside the couch, with terrified looks on their faces. Showbiz turned the gun to Flex and walked up to him just as he put his hands in the air in defeat. His eyes were bloodshot.

"What's all this shit about, Son? Money? Oh, I got about five bands in my pocket. Y'all can have that. It ain't worth dyin' over. Word up." He looked from Showbiz to me.

The strippers were murmuring. They hugged each other and hid their faces from view. Dollar bills littered the floor, along with the two dead men in blood.

Showbiz snatched off his half mask and frowned. "Bitch nigga, you killed my seed and had the audacity to laugh about it. Bitch!" He aimed and started to buss him down.

Shot after shot ripped into Flex's face and throat, and he made a failed attempt to get off the couch. Before he'd come to a standstill, he was dead. Bullets hopped out of Showbiz's .9 millimeter and onto the carpet.

I kneeled and picked them all up, having remembered that our father taught me to do that during hits.

I thought we were on our way out of the house when Showbiz popped the clip out of the pistol and slammed a new one in. He turned his gun on the strippers and let his clip ride once again. I watched him slay them and I felt sick to my stomach. They crawled all over each other, trying to get out of his line of fire, to no avail.

"Yo, come on. Let's make sure ain't nobody else in the house, Kid." He put his mask back over his face and waved for me to follow toward the back of the house.

I picked up all the shells and threw them in my pocket. One glance at the strippers and I felt woozy. I'd never been the type of nigga that could easily body a female. As long as I'd been bussin' my gun, I'd never murdered one. I never saw the reason or purpose. Showbiz had always said that was going to be my downfall in the long run. Whenever I slayed a nigga, it got the best of me for weeks on end, and I couldn't imagine what killing an innocent female would do to my conscious.

The craving came. I needed some Percocet. I needed the high. I was getting sick again.

We made it to the back of the house. Showbiz ran in one room and I another. I flipped the bed before looking under it in search of anybody else. I found nothing. We met back in the hallway where we traveled down the narrow hall, kicking doors in one by one and raiding the rooms on the other side of them.

After not recovering anything, we made our way back toward the kitchen. When were there, I notice that the door to the pantry was closed, so I cocked my foot back and kicked it in. *Whoom!* It flew inward and slammed into the wall.

I nearly lost my breath when I saw the two women huddled together on the pantry floor, hugging one another. As soon as the door had been kicked from its hinges, one of them yelped and screamed.

Showbiz flipped on the light in the little pantry, and when I was able to identify Perjah, I started panic. There she was out in front of the other female with her back to her in protection. They were both kneeling. The other female was crying her eyes out while Perjah looked on, determined to meet her deadly fate.

Showbiz scrunched his face and stepped forward with his pistol. He raised it and aimed it directly at Perjah.

Chapter 7

Before he could squeeze the trigger, I pushed his wrist out of the way. He fired, and his bullet slammed into a five-pound bag of flour. The pantry was filled with the powdery substance. It wafted into the air. Both women were covered by it. The other female began to cry harder. Perjah only hugged her and looked over her shoulder at us.

I stepped in front of Showbiz. "Nah, bruh. Let's go." I couldn't let him kill Perjah. I just couldn't. I felt that we'd already caused her family so much grief. Not that we been the cause of her daughter being paralyzed, but killed her little brother, and five other people in her living room. I had to spare her life. My nose began to run. I was feening for the Percocet at the wrong time.

"Nigga, you out of your muthafucking mind! We gotta kill these two bitches. It's six bodies in the living room. Get the fuck out of my way, bruh!" Showbiz made a move to toss me to the side.

I was bigger and stronger. I refused to be moved. "N'all, Son. Not them. Let's get the fuck out of her. We got who we came to get. It's over." I tried to push him out of the pantry.

Showbiz bussed three times over my shoulder, trying to hit them. They screamed as more dry goods exploded and fell on them. He continued to squeeze his trigger, but there was nothing left but clicks coming from it now, indicating that it was empty. "Kill them bitches, nigga! You tryin' to get us locked up for life! Shoot them hoes!" He demanded, trying to snatch my Uzi from my hand.

I wasn't going. I knocked his hands away and pushed him from me.

He mugged me with hatred and shook his head. "You always do this shit, nigga. You try to save bitches. Bitches gotta catch slugs just like niggas. Now, shoot them bitches. Hurry up!" He looked around as if he was about become hysterical.

Perjah wrapped her arms more protectively around the other female. She looked me in the eyes for a long time before squinting as if something had just clicked in her brain. Her eyes got bucked, then she shook her head. "Please, don't do this. You're better than this. We don't deserve to die."

"Shoot them bitches, lil' bruh. Fuck it. Give me that mufucka then." He reached for the Uzi.

I yanked it away from him and pushed him into the hallway. "Let's go!"

He slammed his fist into the wall. "Fuck! This some bullshit!" He took off running toward the front of the house.

Before I followed him, I looked over my shoulder and into the face of Perjah. We made eye contact. She mouthed the words *thank you*.

I followed Showbiz back to his whip where he stormed away from the curb with the tires screaming.

"I can't believe you just botched that shit, Tristian. Something told me I should've did that shit myself!" He snapped, slamming his hands on the steering wheel. "What the fuck is your problem?"

"Son, I wasn't feeling it. Them broads ain't have shit to do with us slumping Flex. That nigga's dead. Now Maine can rest in peace." I rolled my window down a lil' bit so I could get some fresh air. I was feeling real sick on the stomach. That Mollie that he'd given me wasn't agreeing with my system. I needed to get somewhere and chill. I felt like I was about to lose my mind. I still couldn't believe that Showbiz had been seconds away from killing, Perjah."

"Yo, and Pops think you're fit to run this family after he's gone. Nigga, you ain't fuck one soul in that house tonight. All you did was pick up a bunch of fuckin' shells. Shells from bullets that I'd put into them bodies back there. Then when it was time for you to buss your gun, you ain't do shit but try and save a couple bitches. You're real soft for that shit, Tristian. Word is bond, you soft as fuck."

"Man, fuck you, Showbiz. Everybody ain't murder-hungry like you, nigga. We'd already killed our target. There was no reason to kill all them other people. That was stupid. All you did was get us a bigger page line in the New York Times. I can't see you running the family after Pops is gone either. You'd have every last one of us in prison in no time."

"N'all, nigga, you would! I kill so that there are no more witnesses. You saving them hoes gon' wind up being the downfall of this family. Mark my words, nigga. Matter fact—" He slammed on the brakes and stopped the whip in the middle of the busy street. Cars were blowing their horns before driving around us in irritation. He'd stopped the truck literally in the center of the intersection.

"What the fuck are you doing?" I asked looking over my shoulder.

"Get the fuck out, nigga! You wanna save hoes and shit. Find your way home. I ain't fuckin' with you no more tonight."

"What? Man, you better drop me off where you picked me up."

Showbiz turned to me with a scowl on his face. "Get the fuck out of my whip, Tristian. I ain't playing, nigga."

I frowned and looked him over. "This how you gon' do this shit? You gon' act like a bitch because I ain't let you kill two innocent women?"

He sucked his teeth and lowered his eyes. Cars were blowing their horns loudly. I started to fear the police rolling up and finding me with a pocket full of bullet casings and an Uzi. One that probably had a few bodies. I felt like Showbiz had lost his mind and went over the deep end. I didn't know what he was thinking, and I didn't have time to figure it out.

I opened the door to the whip. "A'ight, then. I'll holler. Take Yo' emotional ass on 'bout yo' business." I slammed the door so hard that it broke the glass.

Showbiz grunted. "Hey, Tristian. Even though you my brother, I can see myself killin' you one of these days. You ain't fit to even be in the runnin' for Pop's seat. You's a soft ass nigga, and one day this blood between us gon' run out." He stepped on the gas and sped away, leaving a bunch of glass behind.

Cars began to drive around me as I ran my way out of the middle of the street, and ultimately back to the crib after finding a twenty-four-hour CVS that filled prescriptions.

* * *

I stayed up that night until the sun rose. I'd taken four of the Percocet thirties, crushed them up, and tooted them line by line. I was high and paranoid of what was to come from the Flex dilemma. Before two in the morning the news was being covered by almost every outlet in New York. They were reporting a mass slaying. Seven dead and two left alive. The seven had been executed in a bloody fashion. They were reporting that two men of color were responsible for the murders and the police were working closely with the witnesses and a sketch artist. I didn't know what that meant for our fate, but I was scared out of my mind. The last place I wanted to wind up was in somebody's prison.

Kalani showed up at about seven o'clock the next morning. She started to beat on the door like a maniac until I answered it in my boxers and a bulletproof vest. My head was pounding, and I felt like I needed to throw up. In my hand was a Glock .40, but I'd neglect d to put the clip in the gun. My mind was that fucked up.

She stepped past the threshold and closed the door behind her. She looked me up and down and rubbed the sides of my face. "What's the matter, Tristian? What did you do? Look at me. What did you do?"

I dry heaved and made a run for the bathroom. I got there, dropped to my knees and hurled my guts at the same time flushing the toilet. I stood up and poured Scope in my mouth, gargling it around, before spitting it into the sink.

Kalani came into the bathroom and rubbed my back. "You killed somebody, Tristian. I can smell it over you. Who was it, baby, and why did they have to go?" She hugged my back and then turned me around so that I was facing her. She was holding my face in her small hands again.

I shook my head. "I ain't kill nobody. It was just a fucked up night." I brushed her hands away from me and walked into my bedroom, sitting on the edge of the bed.

She came all the way into the room and walked over to my dresser. She dipped her finger in the pill dust on top of it and rubbed her finger and thumb together. "What he fuck is this? It better not be coke." She mugged me.

I rubbed my face and sighed. "Yo, why the fuck are you here so early, shorty?" I yawned and stretched my arms above my head.

She touched the tip of her tongue with the pill dust and ran her tongue over her teeth. "N'all, this ain't coke. What the fuck is it, Tristian, seriously?"

"It's Perks. I be needing them joints to relieve the pain. Stop being so damn nosey all the time."

She stepped over to me and stood in my face. "What you call being nosey, I call caring about your silly ass. Now why the fuck are you tooting it like a dope addict? What's the matter with you, Tristian?"

I stood up and bumped her out of the way. "It's way too early to be arguing with you. I gotta get on my grind and figure this shit out for my old man. I got a lot of pieces to put together." I opened the door to my closet and pulled out a gray and black Burberry fit, grabbed my New York fitted cap, and finally a pair of Retro Jordan 13's to complete my ensemble.

"That fool Flex got smoked last night along with a few of the dancers from Low Key's Strip Club. Seeing as how you're acting all out of your mind and shit, I know you had something to do with it. Tell me what's good. You know I'm here for you." She grabbed my wrist.

Ever since I was a young nigga, Kalani had always been the only one in my life that I could open up to and tell my deepest secrets. Most people went to their pastor or Shepard of the church, but I confided in her or my old man. I sighed and lowered my head. "You just can't let things go, can you?"

"Not when it involves you. Now, tell me what's going on, and don't leave nothing out." She stepped in front of me and looked up into my brown eyes.

I shook my head. "Yo, we went and hollered at Flex last night and shit got out of hand. Before he clapped Flex, he clapped some stripper broad in the hall. Shit took off from there. Before it was all done, five people, not counting Flex, were slain. Bruh was about to stroke some other females too when I stopped him. I peeped that one of them was that little girl Brittany's mother. Her name's Perjah. Had I not seen that, I would've let bro do his thing, but I didn't. Now me and that nigga at odds but it is what it is." I walked away from her and threw my clothes on the bed. Then, I went to the dresser and pulled out a fresh wife beater and some boxers. "Why are you over here so early, Kalani?"

"I saw the news. They showed Flex's picture. Then, if that wasn't a giveaway, Showbiz called me early this morning, saying that I need to come over and holler at you. He said that I need to talk some sense into you or you're going to ruin the family. I didn't know what that meant, but I guess I kind of do now." She stepped back in front of me. "I know you're supposed to kill everybody in that house, Tristian. That's the way it goes. Those people killed your nephew. The only way to get your revenge is in blood. After hearing you tell me the story, it sounds like you didn't buss your gun at all. I gotta side with Showbiz on this one." She shook her head and sat on the edge of the bed.

I was taken aback. "The only mufucka in that house who deserved to die was Flex. The strippers, them other niggas, Perjah and that other bitch ain't deserved to get smoked. Showbiz was just on some bullshit, taking lives because he could. That ain't ever been my style and you know that." I grabbed my clothes off the bed, brought them into the bathroom with me, and started the shower.

Kalani, stood up, and shrugged. "I don't know what you saw. Had it been me, I would've bussed my gun until there were no bullet left. That's how it's supposed to be. Had Flex and his ran in on you and Showbiz and let's just say you guys were at you mother's house, he would have killed her and everybody else in the house. That's his track record. His name bring shivers to the goons out in Harlem. Now you run the risk of these bitches that you left alive going to the law on you. The news is already reporting that the witnesses are working closely with a sketch artist. I hope you guys at least had ski masks on, or you're dead meat."

She was giving me a headache. "Look, Kalani, you wasn't there. You ain't see what I saw. I don't know what you would have done if you were in my shoes, but I did what I did, and that's the end of it. You sound like you kissing that nigga's ass more than anything else. My word, sometimes I think you low key got a thing for Showbiz. You like them heartless, rough neck niggas anyway." I curled my lip at her.

She sucked her teeth. "If I wanted to fuck with your brother I could have a long time ago. I done caught how he look at me. He got this habit of squeezing my ass whenever we hug and shit too. I mean, I'd be lying if I said I ain't thought about how it would be to be with him, but I'd never cross you like that. I have more morals than you give me credit for." She rolled her eyes.

"So, you let bruh rub and squeeze on your ass and shit? Huh?"

"Here we go with this shit. Yeah, I have, Tristian, and it ain't no big deal, so don't make it out to be, damn. We ain't even together yet anyway, right?"

"Shorty on the real, I ain't got time to fuck with you right now. You ain't doing shit but giving me a headache. I'm tired of hearing your voice. Shut up." I dropped my vest to the floor and stepped out of my boxers, preparing to get into the shower.

Kalani crossed her arms in front of her chest. "I wouldn't even be wrong if I fucked him, Tristian. The you talk to me, you don't deserve my loyalty or my respect. Besides, when I fell for your ass, you were a street nigga. I don't know what you done morphed into ever since that lil' bitch got you shot up. It seemed like you're stressing more about her than you are about your own nephew getting killed. Your priorities are backwards as a muthafucka."

I stepped out of the show and leaned into the bathroom door. "Shorty, leave my crib."

"What?" she looked offended.

"You heard me. Get the fuck out my crib. I ain't feeling you right now. I need to get my head together and you ain't doin' shit right now but adding to my stress level. I'll holler at you when I get my mind right."

"I ain't goin' nowhere. You don't run shit. I ain't worried about you doing nothing to either. You ain't even have the balls to buss your gun over your nephew. I know you ain't gon' do shit to me." She had the nerve to up her hand.

As soon as she had, I backhanded her ass so fast that I didn't even realize I had until she fell with a loud thump on the floor. "Get the fuck out my crib, Kalani. It seem like you always tryin' to push me to the point where I gotta whoop yo' ass. I'm not trying to be going through this shit with you. I got too much on my plate."

She stood, holding her face. "You hit like a bitch, nigga. I see why that G shit ain't in you no more. Your turning soft. Maybe I should go and fuck your brother. At least then I wouldn't be bumping pussies with a pussy." She hauled off and smacked me as hard as she could. She pushed me in the chest, causing me to fall over the rim of the tub before she took off running through the house. "You a bitch, Tristian!"

I had a tough time regaining my footing. When I did, I was in hot pursuit of her. I found her in the living room with my Louisville Slugger. "Bitch, you done lost your rabid ass mind or something?"

She choked up on the bat and clenched her teeth. "Come on, muthafucka, 'cuz I ain't goin' nowhere. I'ma beat the bitch out of you with this bat. Bring yo' naked ass on." She rushed forward and swung the bat, clashing it into my forearm before cocking it back and whacking me again across the shoulder.

Kalani had been an all-state first batsmen in high school, so she knew a little bit about swinging a bat. The shot to my forearm hurt so bad that I hollered out in pain. While I was gathering myself, that's when she swung and whacked me across the shoulder. Those were the only blows that I took because after that, I grabbed her the throat and lifted her all the way into the air and slammed her down on top of my table, breaking it and kicking her lil' ass out cold. I never liked putting my hands on her, but ever since we'd been together, it seemed like that's all she made me do. I left her ass right on top of the table, then took my shower.

When I came out, she was still in the living room, sitting with her knees to her chest and her arms wrapped around them, looking up at me. She stood up. "I'm sorry for what I did, Tristian. You just make me so mad at times. I think you're getting too soft, so sometimes I gotta test you to see where your heart is. Do you forgive me?" She walked over to me and wrapped her arms around my naked body before falling to her knees, grabbing my piece to stroke it.

I knocked her hand away and grabbed her up by the hair. She shrieked and fought against me as I led her to the front of the house, toward the door, opening it. "Shorty, holler at me when you get your shit together." I threw onto the stood and got ready to close the door.

She rushed to it and crashed it with her shoulder. "Tristian, if you throw me out like this, you're going to regret it! I swear you're going to regret it!" she promised with tears flowing down her cheeks.

I reached through the crack of the door and pushed her face until she cleared the space. Then, I closed the door. She went on a rant for about twenty minutes about what she was going to do. I ignored that shit and got dressed. It was time I got on my grind and figured my life out. After her car screeched away from the curb, I tooted two more pills and got my mind together.

Chapter 8

It was a week later, and I'd agreed to meet up with Miguel after I left my school for the day. It was hot, and kind of breezy when I pulled up on him in the parking lot. He was there talking to an Asian female that was built like a sista. When he saw my truck roll up, they exchanged hugs and then he walked over and pulled on my passenger's door handle to get in.

"What's good, big bro? What's the word for the day?" He asked, pulling out a Dutch and sparking it.

We really ain't have much to do on this way. I was wondering why he'd called me out here to meet up. "You tell me what the word? You know me and you don't even get down like this."

He laughed and nodded. "Right, right. Yeah, shit's crazy. But no matter what we've been through, we're still brothers. We share the same blood, Tristian. Sooner or later, we gon' have to deal with each other, so why not more sooner than later?"

"Anyway, what it is? Why the fuck you wanted to meet up? You made it seem important."

"I got a lick that can bring us at least two million in cash and about a million in heroin too. I need your help with it. I wanted to holler at Showbiz but bruh ain't fuckin' with me right now. He said he handlin' his own business, so he can take a seat on the throne. That he ain't got no brothers right now. Whatever that means."

A pretty Mexican chick stepped out of the Subway and got into the passenger's seat of his gray Range Rover Sport that my father bought him for his eighteenth birthday. My father also bought the truck that I was driving. He'd given it to me for my twenty-first birthday.

"Yeah, what's good with this lick? Who put you up on it?"

He pointed with his head toward his truck. "That's my lil' bitch right there. She just found out that she's pregnant with my kid. Her uncle fuck with Diablo's cats out in Mexico City, Mexico. She say that nigga gon' be out here in New York for the weekend. He got two million in cash and a million in Black Tar heroin. We can hit that lick and be three million to the good. What do you say?"

"Nah, I'll pass. I don't trust you, lil' dawg. You've always been a fuck nigga to me. Plus, your heart ain't right. Deep down, you ain't nothin' but a wolf with Vega skin covering you."

His face turned beet red right away. "I knew I shouldn't have come to you, Tristian. I knew running this shit by you was going to be a big mistake. But that's cool though because when I get that throne, I'ma make you kiss my feet, nigga. You and every Black muthafucka that I want. That's why I hate you monkeys. Y'all ain't—"

Bam! I bussed him right in his mouth, jumped out of my truck and ran around to the other side to open the door, causing him to fall out and into the parking lot.

He held his mouth with blood running through his fingers. I'ma kill you one day, Tristian. I swear on my mother, I'ma kill yo' bitch ass one day." He slowly made his way to his feet.

His baby's mother rushed out of his truck to him. She wrapped her arms around him and gave me an angry look. She stomped her foot at me. "This is the asshole you wanted to help you rob my uncle, Miguel?" she asked him in Spanish.

He nodded and made his way to his driver's side door. "Fuck that nigger, baby. When I become king, he's the first monkey I'm going to kill. I swear that on our kid," he returned in Spanish.

I laughed at both, jumped in my truck and rolled away. On my way out of the parking lot, I received a text from Perjah. She said that we needed to talk right away, and that she needed me to meet up with her at the Harbor House Women's Shelter which was down the street from Mount Sinai. I was completely taken off guard. I didn't know how to respond.

On one hand, I really wanted to have a sit down with her because I was concerned not only about Brittany, but about her as well. We'd not only wounded her daughter for life but had recently taken the life of her brother. I couldn't imagine what she was going through. Next to that, I worried that meeting with her could've been a setup. We'd locked eyes the night of the murders. I had a gut feeling that she'd recognized me. If that was the case, then I was surely rolling the dice with my life. She could have anything up her sleeve. Even with that realization something drew me toward her. I felt that I just had to see this woman. I never remembered having felt this pull toward anybody in my entire life.

* * *

The Harbor House had been an old Boys and Girls club that had been converted into a battered women's shelter. It was a two two-story, red bricked building with a huge parking lot. When I got there, Perjah was waiting in front of the building. She ran her fingers through her curly hair and paced until I beeped the horn and rolled in front of her.

She walked up to my ruck and looked in the back windows, and then at me through the passenger's window. She knocked on the glass, so I rolled it down. "Tristian, I know that was you the other night. We need to talk because I don't know what to do." She wound up getting into my truck.

I drove her to the lakefront where I parked, and we got out and walked along the walkway beside the lake.

She had bags under her eyes. Her hair though very curly was a little all over the place. She looked thinner. "First my daughter and now my little brother, Tristian. What does your family have against mine?" She asked with watery eyes.

I tossed her up against the gate that separated us from the water, and kicked he legs apart. I searched her then turned her around and pulled her shirt away from her chest in search of a wire. After finding none, I even took her earrings out and   tossed them into the lake.

"Hey, what are you doing?" She hollered angrily.

"I don't know what the fuck you tryin' to pull. You called me out the blue wanting to meet. What am I to think?"

She knocked my hands away from her and pushed me out of her face, fixing her clothes. "I'm not a fucking snitch. That's not in me. If I was, you'd be in prison already. You can bet your bottom dollar on that." She wiped her mouth. "Now, what does your family have against mine? I deserve to know. I just lost my brother and my daughter is still in the hospital. Why are you guys targeting us?"

I looked over her shoulder at the water. I watched the waves crash into each other before splashing loudly. "Flex killed my nephew the same day that Brittany and I were shot. My nephew was only six years old."

"Wait, so is that what this is all about?" She asked, looked up at me.

"Yeah, your brother was a dirty nigga. Him and my brother, I guess, had a lot of bad blood from their dealings in the streets. One thing led to another and we've been having funerals on both sides ever since. Now that Flex is gone, it could be good. The score is settled." I walked away from her. I felt we looked crazy just standing there in the middle of the board-walk.

Perjah jogged to catch up to me. "I don't know what really happened between those two, but I just wanted to thank you for saving my life the other night. You saved mine and my nieces lives, and you didn't have to do that. I feel like I owe you."

I shook my head as a bunch of crows flew across the sky. "You don't owe me nothin', Perjah. You didn't deserve to die and neither did those other women, it's too late to cry about that now, so let's not."

"Tristian, if he would've killed me, my daughter would've had nobody to take care of her. She would be out in this cold world all alone. I thank you for what you've done. You have to let me repay you. I'll do anything."

"You wanna repay me? All you gotta do is let me be a part of you and Brittany's life. Let me pay her medical bills. Let me stand by your side and protect you from whatever else is out there. I'm sure your brother had more enemies than my brother. Allow me to protect you from them at all cost.

I didn't know what I was saying fully. All I knew was that I meant it. I didn't know what was about to happen to her or Brittany. I knew how Showbiz got down. He would come back eventually to finish the job.

Perjah bit her fingernail. "You think he has more enemies that will come for us? I mean, I've never hurt anybody in my life, and Brittany is just a little girl. It's not fair. All we want to do is live our lives." Her voice began to crack. She blinked tears and started to shake.

I pulled her into my embrace. "Perjah, I'm not gon' let nothing happen to you or her. You got my word on that. I'd rather die first. You hear me?"

She nodded then shook her head. "N'all. Screw that. I have a registered gun. I won't go down without a fight. If somebody wants to harm us, they're going to have to kill me first. I won't let me and my daughter reach harm again. I just won't." She beat her fists on my chest and broke down sobbing.

I squeezed her tighter and scanned the lakefront. It was mostly deserted that the time. There were a few people laying on their stomachs on the sand. There were a few white children flying kites and three college aged white girls were setting up a volleyball net.

Perjah came from under my arm and wiped her face. "I don't know if I can trust you, Tristian. If your brother is as rotten as he is, who's to say that somewhere down the line it won't surface in you? All that me and Brittany have is each other." She bit into her lower lip and pulled a tuft of her hair behind her left ear. Her curly hair blew in the wind.

I exhaled, grabbed both of her wrists, and looked down into her beautiful face. "Perjah, all I'm asking is that you give me a chance to prove myself to you two. I can see that you are a very strong and independent woman. I can tell that you are used to being on your own and having to stand up for yourself. I get that. I want to help you. Just let me do what I can. I don't mind you watch me closely and put everything that I provide under a figurative microscope. That's your right. But you'll see that my heart is genuine." I brushed her hair out of her face once again. There was a steady flow of wind that caused her hair to fly all over the place. "Where have you been staying since the murders took place?"

"At the Super Eight Motel about three blocks over from Mount Sinai. Some of the women that frequent the shelter reside there from time to time. It's not the best, nor the safest, but it's all I can afford right now. I can't go back to the house knowing what took place there. Besides, the local authorities have been all over the place every single day."

I felt bad for her. I could see the bags forming under her eyes. I could tell that she hadn't had a good night's sleep in probably a month or so. "Well, will you please allow for me to put you up in a better hotel? There is the Waldorf Astoria about a mile away from the hospital, or maybe you'd prefer the W. You can pick either one, but I can't have you staying in some motel. That ain't cool, nor is it safe."

She lowered her head and then looked up at me. "No. Thank you for offering, but I've thought it out. I've not had any problems so far, and I run into any, I know how to defend myself. I'm from Harlem. I grew up fighting my whole life. Nothing has ever been easy for me. I can't allow some man to come in and save the day. I have to stand on my own two feet as a woman."

I held her wrists and looked into her pretty eyes. While I respected everything she was saying, because I'd only heard those words come from my mother's mouth, at the time I didn't agree to them. I didn't feel like she honestly understood what she was up against. She was a witness to a brutal massacre that Showbiz had enforced. I knew from experience that she was living on borrowed time. My family didn't do loose ends. She was a throw at my father's throne, and because of that, she was an enemy to the Vegas.

"Alright, look." I reached into my pocket and pulled out ten one hundred-dollar bills and tried to hand them to her. "At least take this band. You can put yourself up in any place you'd like. Just get the hell out of that one." I placed her face into my right hand and stroked her cheek with my thumb. "I just need to make sure you're good. You have to stay in the best position possible, if not for yourself, then for Brittany." I thought it would be smart to throw that last dig in there to remind her that it wasn't just about her, but her daughter as well.

She pushed the money away. "And while I'm extremely flattered by your generosity, I'm going to have to decline it. I'll figure things out. I've never been one to accept a handout. I really do appreciate you though. It takes one hell of a man to do what you're doing. In the morning, I'll probably introduce you to Brittany. You need to know that this is big for me. I am extremely overprotective of my daughter. The circumstances surrounding all of this is very controversial, but there is something about you that tells my heart that it's okay. I'm willing to follow my gut on this one. I only pray to God that you are who you're making yourself out to be, so I'll take the next three Monday mornings, let's say to get myself together."

I nodded and smiled. "That sounds good. I'll be between classes at the time. I'll have about an hour to properly get to know her. Thank you for this opportunity." I opened my arms for her to walk into them. When she did, I felt like an angel on the verge of getting its wings.

Chapter 9

Over the next couple of days, I wound up hitting the books hard and handling as much of my classwork online. I couldn't seem to get Perjah or Brittany off my mind, no matter how hard I tried. I was thinking about it so much that the priorities with my father had fell to the back of my mind. I had yet to come up with a solid plan of action. With everything going on in my life, I didn't know when I would get around to it. I would honestly say that I was about to lose my drive and focus earning my father's throne. I'd always wanted something different anyway. I didn't want to be on the run from the law my entire life or looking over my shoulder forever. To me, that wasn't living. When a man chose to put his foot into the underworld of narcotics and war, there was so much that came with it. Money was the last thing. It wasn't all glitz and glamour as they made it to be in movies. The battle of supremacy would cost you the lives of your family or anyone you loved. I wanted to go another way.

I wanted to be legit. To conquer the world the righteous way, by outthinking other businessmen and politicians. I didn't want to be enslaved by the drug trade as many people had before me. The game was designed to allure, enslave and destroy. Most were allured by the hustlers they saw in their foreign whips, jewelry, bad women and pulls of money. They saw an object of what they wanted to become, and they could obtain the hustler's position by doing exactly what they were, not knowing that the hustler was nothing more than a pawn. A mouse trap. He was put in a place to allure a mass amount of poor and struggling men. Once they were baited into the realm, they found themselves trapped or enslaved by the game. They'd been given enough opportunity to survive long enough in the game to allure others. But as soon as their short clock ran out, nine times out of ten they were destroyed by either prison or death.

I was smart enough to know that real hustlers didn't hustle in the hood. They owned acres and acres of poppy and coco leaf fields. They owned private jets and shipped tons of heroin and cocaine each month. They didn't operate in the sale of petty ass kilos. They dealt with millions of dollars at a time, not thousands. These men were considered the power pieces on the board. Every other hustler under them were nothing more than pawns that had an inevitability to death and destruction.

They were destined to lose unless they were able to reach the top of the panicle— the status that my father had. To reach such a status, you had to had to play the political game and you had to play it quite well. Palms had to be greased and favors had to be handed out across the board. My father always said that everybody gets used in the game. If you cannot be used, you're worthless and nothing more than trash. The more power your usage is, the higher you extend. You must transcend the slums because nobody cares about the poor and the disenfranchised. You must outthink them to make them care.

* * *

I woke up the following Sunday morning to find Showbiz standing over me with two .40s in his hands. "Tristian get yo' lil' ass up, nigga. I wanna show you why this muthafuckin' throne is about to be mine, and not even Pops can deny me of this shit." He smiled, looking down at me.

I sat up in bed and squeezed my eyelids tight. I had a headache that was pounding like crazy. It was so bad that I wanted to throw up. I slid my hand under my pillow and grabbed my bottle of pills. They were calling me. I needed to treat my nose before I went anywhere with him. "How the fuck you get in my crib, nigga?" I slid out of the bed and made my way into the bathroom. I closed the door and crushed three pills on the sink before tooting them.

"Never mind that shit. Just get dressed and come fuck with me. I got something I gotta show you, so you can bow down to my gangsta." He laughed again. "Hurry up, nigga. Time is money."

I got dressed, grabbed my .9 millimeter and slid it onto my waist before pulling my shirt over it. When I stepped outside, I saw that Showbiz had a strawberry Rolls Royce sitting in front of my brownstone. It was sitting on twenty-eight-inch gold rims. The paint looked wet as if it was freshly done. There were specks of Louis Vuitton emblems inside of it. I couldn't help but to buck my eyes. Showbiz had always been one for fresh whips that fucked the game up. He was one of those flashy dudes that loved the spotlight. I could only imagine what our family would look like with him seated on the throne of the Vegas.

When he pulled away from the curb, I looked over at him and he smiled with a mouth full of golds. It was the first time that I noticed he'd gotten his teeth done. "Kid, what's with this flashy ass ride? You tryin' to get indicted or something?" I asked, pulling on my nose. I felt my pills kicking in. I felt breezy and numb at the same time.

"Not as long as Shapiro workin' for me when Pops step down. I'm thinking of making him my personal lawyer, so he can just focus on me. I'll get a whole firm to make sure y'all straight and shit. Nah'mean?" He laughed. "Far as the whip go, I deserve this bitch. This courtesy of my niggas out in DC." Showbiz loved fucking around in Washington DC. I'd been out there a couple of times with him, but I found them niggas to be grimy, disrespectful, arrogant and more than a few were downlow homo thugs. I ain't ever been the time to knock a nigga for how they got down, but I didn't like surprises or that sneaky shit. I never liked going out there with him, but it was his second home in the States.

"So, where are you taking me, Kid? What's this shit you talking about Pops gon' have to give you the throne?"

He cheesed. "Oh, you finna see in a minute. Just lean back and listen to the music. We'll be there shortly."

I did just that after sending Perjah a text, telling her to have a good morning and that I was thinking about her. She responded with a thank you and told me to have a good morning as well. I don't know why, but those few words from her made me feel good as hell.

* * *

"Ta da, muthafucka. This how you get down when you tryin' to take over a muthfucking throne. Don't ask me how I did it, just know that I handled muthafuckin' business!" Showbiz hollered.

I walked further into the basement. My eyes adjusted to a red lightbulb to allow me to see in front of me. We were inside the bottom of a two-story building in Newark, New Jersey. It was hot and stuffy down there. It smelled like strong piss and sweat. The stench was so strong that I covered my nose briefly. In the center of the basement was both Chulo and Wisin. They had silver duct tape wrapped around their arms, wrists and ankles. In their mouths was a red rag. Both men had sweat dripping from their faces. Their clothes were saturated in their fluids. Behind them were four of Showbiz's riders. They had red rags around their necks, and AK-47s in their hands, laid against their shoulders.

"Showbiz, what have you done, big bruh?" I circled the men and cringed. They smelled like they'd used the bathroom on themselves more than once.

He smacked Chulo on the back of the head. "Pops said that we needed to take over the Red Hook Houses, right?"

I sighed. "Right?"

"Well, the Gomez brothers run the Red Hook Houses. But guess who run them though?" He laughed. "Same old story, time and time again. Umm, umm, ummph." He shook his head.

"Who run them, Showbiz?" I already had a smart-ass answer, but I figured I'd humor him anyway. I was still trying to wrap my head around the fact that he'd been able to snatch up both the Gomez brothers in such a short amount of time. Maybe he was more fit for my Pops' throne than I was. I didn't even know if I wanted it because of what it represented. I wasn't so sure that I wanted the responsibility of our entire bloodline on my shoulders. I didn't want to be weighed down. I wanted so much more out of life than that position had to offer.

"Pussy, Tristian. All it took was for me to put some of our Cuban cousins on these fuck boys, lure them out of their hiding places and away from their safety zones. Tisk, tisk, tisk." He stepped next to me and put his arm around my shoulder and leaned close to my ear. "By the way, I found out where both bitches that you kept alive lay their heads. After I'm finished securing this throne, I'ma make sure that I right your wrongs. You know the rules of the game, Tristian. I can't allow for them hoes to live. It is what it is." He snickered and patted me on the back. Then, he took the pistol off his hip and pressed it to Wisin's forehead. Afterward, he snatched the rag out of his mouth. "Say, fuck nigga. Y'all been over there getting money for about five straight years now. If you had to put a number on how much cash your family has in the safe, what number would that be?" He cocked the hammer back.

Wisin scrunched his face. "Fuck you, Showbiz. Fuck all you Vegas. When my father gets a hold of this news, you'll be sorry. You can kiss my—"

Boom.

Showbiz popped him once in the right kneecap, blowing it from his leg. His gun was left smoking.

The scent of gunpowder entered the basement. My ears were ringing. I could almost smell burnt flesh from the bullet penetrating his body.

Wisin hopped around in the chair and hollered at the top of his lungs. He started to curse Showbiz out in Spanish. Spit flew from his mouth as he called him every curse word in the book.

Showbiz took a step back and lit a weed-filled cigar. He blew the smoke into Wisin's face and grunted. "Whenever you done making all that muthafuckin' noise, you gon' tell me what I wanna know and where to find this cash. He took another pull off the blunt. "You only got one more knee cap. You feel me?" He stepped forward with the gun extended toward Wisin's knee.

While I watched the scene play before my eyes, I wasn't there mentally. I was thinking about the things that Showbiz whispered to me regarding Perjah and her niece. I had to find a way to shake him and get to her before something horrible happened that I couldn't prevent. As much as I loved my brother, at times I felt like I truly hated him.

Boom.

Showbiz had blown off Wisin's left kneecap. It sent blood running down his calf. He shit on himself and lowered his head in defeat. Sweat dripped of his chin. "I don't give a fuck how many bullets you put in me, showbiz, I ain't tellin' you shit. My pride and my love for my family won't allow it." He was struggling to talk. I could tell the pain was getting the better of him.

Showbiz nodded. "You know what? I respect that. A man of pride. Hmm. That's what's up." He stepped forward and crashed the fiery end of the of the blunt into Chulo's face.

Chulo flopped around in his chair. He screamed into the gag and forced snot out of his nose. His chair fell on its side. Showbiz's men stepped up to him and aimed their AKs at his chest awaiting the word to end dude's life.

Showbiz stepped on his neck with his Timberland boot. He pointed his gun at him. "Tell me something, Wisin. How much do you love your lil' brother?"

Wisin swallowed, looking at the scene from the corner of his eyes. There was a puddle of blood surrounding his chair. He winced in pain, shaking his head. "Ten million."

A big smile crept across Showbiz's face. He took a step back and walked over to Wisin, laying his hand on his shoulder. "Now, we're getting somewhere. I'll need an address, the safe's codes and a full layout of the spot we'll be retrieving this cash from. The longer you take, the more you'll bleed."

* * *

Wisin and Chulo were nothing more than your average run of the mill dope boys who kept large sums of money at their baby mother's houses, not knowing that an idiotic move like that always put their own people in jeopardy. I never understood how some of the things that were so obvious about the game; most hustlers missed.

After an hour, Wisin finally gave up all the information, and Showbiz and I were crashing through the patio door of where him and his baby mother laid their heads.

Wisin's baby mother had been sitting in the den braiding their daughter's hair. Startled, she jumped up, screaming as Showbiz ran up on her, smacking her to the floor.

"Bitch, take me upstairs to the safe. Let's go." He hollered, dragging her by her hair as she kicked her legs wildly.

Their five-year-old daughter stood in the middle of the floor with her hands against her face, hair half done. "Mommy! Mommy!" She screamed as she reached out for her mother.

Showbiz extended his pistol toward her. "Shut that lil' bitch up, bruh, before I stank her lil' loud ass." He warned.

I scooped the little girl into my arms and took her into the open room I saw. I sat her on the bed and spoke to her in Spanish. "Calm down, lil' lady. You and your mother are going to be okay if you stay quiet. Understand me?"

She nodded in agreeance. "Please don't let that man hurt my mommy." She looked up at me with tears in her eyes, threatening to escape her.

"Listen to me; stay in here and don't come out until your mother comes down and gets you. If you come out of this room, it's going to be trouble. This is your first and only warning. Understand?"

She nodded as her lips trembled and tears continued to fall from her brown eyes.

I stood up, looking down on her, shaking my head. I closed the door behind me, listening to the commotion I heard upstairs. It sounded like Showbiz was beating ol' girl senseless.

I skipped up the stairs two at a time and ran down the hallway. I found them in the third bedroom to the right of the hallway.

Showbiz had straddled her and was slamming the handle of his gun into her forehead repeatedly. I saw that she also held a .380 in her hand.

"Punk. Bitch. You. Thought. It. Was. Sweet!" He slammed the handle harder and harder into her head until she was knocked out cold. He wiped the blood on her nightgown and stood up. "This bitch had the nerve to pull that muthafucka out of her hair. Can you believe that shit?" He had wild eyes.

Wisin's baby's mother's head was split wide open with blood oozing out of her wounds like thick, red syrup. She jerked on the carpet and kicked her left leg over and over with her eyes wide open.

"She's dying, bruh. Look at her. She's dying." I kneeled beside her, not knowing what to do or if there was something that I should've expected when fuckin' with Showbiz.

He waved her off. "Fuck that bitch. She tried me and that's what happened. Life goes on. Grabbed that other lil' bitch and bring her up here. If this nigga Wisin doesn't tell me where this money is, I'm slump her lil' ass too." He pulled out his phone. "Aye, Chulito, put that nigga on the phone."

I took the stairs in a hurry. When I got to the room where I'd left the little girl, she was there with her face in her arms, crying her little heart out. I closed the door behind me and spoke to her in Spanish.

"Hey, Princess. Get up. We gotta put some clothes on you. Come on."

She was only dressed in a thin white gown that fell to her ankles. I wanted her to at least put on a pair of pants and shoes before I got her out of the house. I wasn't about to let Showbiz kill another innocent person. Especially not a little kid. So, I rushed around the room until I found her a pair of shoes that were obviously hers, and a pair of Jordache jeans. As quickly as I could, I dressed her while she cried and asked where her mother was.

"She's upstairs, but I have to get you dressed and out of the house before the scary man tries to hurt you. We have to hurry up." I pulled up her pants and buttoned them. Then, I grabbed her little wrists and led her to the window of the room. I opened it and looked down at her. "I'm going to lower you down. I want you to sit up against the side of the house until you count to a hundred. Can you count to a hundred?"

She nodded with tears running down her face. "Yes. I can count to a hundred."

"Okay. Sit against the house until you count to a hundred. Then, I want you to get up and run to the neighbor's and tell them that your mommy told you to come over because she's on her way. Can you do that?"

She nodded once again. "But is my mommy going to be okay?" She whined.

Whoom.

Showbiz kicked in the door, causing the little girl to scream. He walked over and put the pun against her nose. Then, he took her to the bed where she kicked like crazy. "What the fuck was taking you so long, Tristian?"

"I was on my way upstairs, damn. Chill." I walked beside the bed and watched as he pressed the barrel harder into her nose.

"You see this shit, Wisin? Play with me, nigga, and I'll stank this lil' bitch. Where's the money?" he hollered into the screen of the phone.

Wisin took one look and gave up all the locations around the house. Showbiz tied the girl up as we unloaded the money into big black trash bags and stuffed as much of it as we could into the trunk of the car before filling up the backseats. When we were through, the house looked destroyed.

We were already loaded into the car with me behind the wheel when Showbiz broke out of the car and went back into the house. "I'll be right back. You wait here," he ordered.

I sat, dumbfounded. I looked into my rearview mirror, praying we would be able to make it out of this situation. I couldn't, for the life of me, think of what he'd possibly needed from that house. That was until I heard a loud pop. As soon as I did, I opened the driver's side door and was about to go in after him, but I knew it was too late. He'd killed her. Once against, I felt like I'd allowed for my brother, the devil, to take another innocent life, just because he wanted to.

He jumped back in the car with an angry scowl on his face. "Let's ride. We gotta count this money to make sure it's the amount that Wisin said it was. It is it, then I can kill them niggas and move in on the Red Hook Houses. I should be able to make that additional five mill in no time. Pops don't know who he fuckin' with. I was born to be a king." He lowered his eyes and crossed his chest with the sign of the crucifix.

* * *

It took us six hours and two money machines to confirm the amount of $10,500,00 in cash from Wisin. Showbiz was out of his mind with glee. He continued to talk about him being the king and taking over New York, then eventually the world.

My mind was somewhere else. Not only was I craving my pills, but I was sick over the little girl. I needed to take my mind off her and off reality. I wanted to hit up Perjah, but it was two in the morning. I didn't know how she would take to me calling her so late. I didn't want to scare her off or make our relationship take two steps back by overstepping my bounds. So, I settled and did something I knew I shouldn't have. I called Kalani and told her to come over to my crib ASAP. She said she'd be on her while, and while I waited for her, I got good and high. I crushed four Percocet and tooted them. I was taking more and more of the drug to get me to feel as good as I had in the beginning, and that scared me some. It was getting so bad that I couldn't go more than an hour at a time without renewing my high. I didn't, I'd feel so sick that I'd throw up and curl up on the floor with sever cramps in my abdomen. As long as I had those pills in my system, I was good. I felt happy and free, and more like myself.

I opened the front door to my crib and there was Kalani, standing on the stoop with the rain pouring hard behind her. She was dressed in a long leather trench coat by Marc Jacobs. She looked me up and down and pursed her lips. "So, you think whenever you call me I'm just gon' come running at the drop of a hat?"

I grabbed her by the hair and pulled her into the hallway. Picked her lil' ass up and bit into her neck, sucking on it hard. She yelped and moaned into my mouth. I gripped her chubby ass cheeks. "You gon' do what the fuck I tell you to do. Don't get shit twisted."

We wound up in the bedroom. I ripped her coat from her to expose her purple, see-through lingerie. I snatched the panties from her and did the same with the bra before pushing her breasts together, sucking on one nipple and then the other. Pulling them with my teeth. At the same time, I kicked my boxers off. My dick was rock hard. The pills had me riled.

With her knees to her chest, I licked up and down her slit loudly. Then, I sucked on her pearl tongue and slurped it into my mouth.

She bucked on the bed. "Aww, shit, Tristian. I missed you so much, baby. I want you to fuck me as hard as you can." She whimpered, sucking her finger into her mouth.

"Shut up, Kalani. Just be quiet and let me do everything." Even though I was going down on her, I was imagining she was Perjah. I don't know why her image came into my mind, but it did, and I ran with it. I had me hornier than a teenager on Viagra.

I remembered how thick her thighs were. The scent of her. Her pretty face. The way she'd turned down the money. All of it affected me in a way that I couldn't understand. I ran two fingers in and out of Kalani's pussy and continued to suck on her clit. She humped into my face.

She wrapped her legs around my shoulders and came all over my mouth. "Ah, fuck, Tristian! You always doin' me like this." She lifted her right leg up and laid on her back.

I got between her legs and rubbed my head up and down her wet slit before slipping into her tightness and slammed home. I felt her heat surrounding my dick. It felt like the first time.

I wondered how it would feel to be intimate with Perjah. Would she be able to take all my inches? Would she scratch up my back? How would her moans sound? What would she smell like during and after our session? Because she was so independent, would she prefer to be on top and in control? Either way, I would've been happy with her.

I felt Kalani's nails digging into my back. "Fuck me, Tristian. Fuck me hard like an animal." She humped into me, to force my piece further into her slot.

I cuffed her calf muscle and got to pounding that pussy out. Our skins slapped against one another. My abs tightened, and I could feel my head pushing through her silky inner walls.

The heat was enough to push me over the edge almost immediately. The pills increased my stamina and made me yearn for more. I leaned down and kissed all over her neck while my ass rose and fell, driving into the deepest regions of her gardens.

"Yes, Tristian. Yes. Fuck me. Fuck me. Fuck me so, so good!" She whimpered with her ankle over my shoulder.

The headboard slammed into the wall, making a loud, constant bang. I searched the depths of her sex in search for her hidden G spot that I never had a problem hitting. As long as I drove into her from an angle, I couldn't miss. I tightened my grip on her calf and did exactly that, fucking her as hard as I could while imagining her being Perjah. Her soft voice. Her pretty brown eyes. The way I felt while I held her in my arms. I could even remember the feel of her tears on my fingertips as I brushed them away. The feel of her hot tears on my neck as she laid her face within the crux of my neck.

I sped up the pace and got to hitting Kalani so hard that she was screaming to slow down. "Wait, Tristian! Wait! Aww shit! Aww shit! Take it easy! It's. It's. Aww-shit!" She started to shake under me.

I could feel the walls of her vagina clamping around my dick. I placed both thighs on my shoulders and kept going with my eyes closed tight. Her juices dripped off my balls and onto the silk sheets below us. "Un. Damn, this pussy good." I huffed and flipped her onto her stomach, pulling her up to her knees.

Once she was there, I slid back in and grabbed her hips. I loved fucking Kalani from the back because she was so thick. Her ass cheeks would crash into my stomach muscles and jiggle for a split second. She had this way of milking me from this angle that drove me nuts. On top of that, I liked to rub all over her ass. Sometimes, I leaned forward, so I could kiss it and lick around her rosebud. This was one those times.

I stopped in mid-stroke, pulled her cheeks apart, and licked between them. It tasted like her pussy juice and sweat. I bit into her cheeks and slid back into her, fucking her like an animal. "Give me this shit! Twerk on this dick, baby," I groaned, fucking her as hard as I could.

"Uhh-aww! Tristian! Tristian! You. Killing. Me!" She slammed back into me repeatedly, looking back at me with her mouth wide open.

I pulled her hair and continued to pump, watching my pipe go in and out of her at full speed. Her pussy opened and closed around it as always. Her asshole sucked at me. I saw the way her thick thighs jiggled every time she crashed against me, and it was too much. I pulled back on her hair and dumped my seed deep inside her belly and kept right on fucking. The Percocet was taking over.

Kalani fell to her stomach and held her ass cheeks open for me while pinching and tweaking her glistening clitoris. "Fuck my ass, Tristian, like you used to when we were in school. I miss that. I need you to fuck my ass, baby." She rose to her knees again and laid her face on the bed.

I rubbed my dick against her crease to lubricate it with the juices that were pouring out of her like a geyser. As soon as it was shining and dripping in her essence, I placed it on her crinkle and slowly pushed it in.

She closed her eyes and ran her tongue around her lips. Her back arched. "Holy fuck, that's a lot of meat, daddy," she said. "I need it though. I fucked up."

I slammed into her and started to pull him in and out of her tight fit. It felt hotter than ever in ass. I could feel her anal walls trying to push me out of her, but I fought against the resistance and picked up a nice pace, waxing that ass.

"Un. Un. Un. I love it. Yes. Yes. Fuck it, harder, Tristian!" She bounced backward,

I held her titties and worked her over. It was feeling so good, so tight and her sounds were getting to my dick because it got harder and harder. I wanted to cum in her so bad. The way her ass jiggled was a trigger. I smacked it hard twice and kept on dicking her down.

She grabbed a fistful of the sheets and squeezed her eyes shut. "It's so good! Fuck me, Showbiz! Fuck me! Aww, Juanito!" As soon as that name came out of her mouth, her eyes popped open. She looked back at me with them bugged out of her head.

I kept fucking. I was too close to cumming. I had to get my seed out of me. "I heard you, bitch!" I dug my nails into her ass and fucked her harder than I ever had.

She fell on her stomach and I kept killing her ass. "I'm sorry! I didn't. Uh! Didn't mean to! Fuck. Him. I'm. Sorry. Please!" She whimpered with her face rubbing against the sheets.

I grabbed her hair and lifted her thigh onto my forearm and really dug into her ass from that angle. I was deep into her bowels with no mercy. I smashed her until I came. Then, I pulled out and bussed all over her lower back and ass cheeks, smearing it around with my dick head. I jumped out of the bed and wiped the sweat off my forehead. My chest was heaving. "So, you fucked Showbiz, huh?"

She curled up into fetal position and nodded. "I'm sorry, Tristian. I was mad at you. We got to drinking, and he made me sit on his lap. After that he started sucking on my neck and you know that's my trigger. One thing led to another, and it just happened. I'm sorry. I still wanna be your wife." She took a deep breath and exhaled slowly before sitting up.

I felt betrayed and relieved at the same time. I guess a part of me knew that, Kalani had been attracted to Showbiz ever since we were in high school. They had this lil' habit of flirting back and forth with each other but I never paid it that much of mind. I knew that Showbiz would fuck any bitch that opened her legs. He didn't care if she was your wife or not. That's just how he was.

I honestly cared about Kalani, and I was feeling guilty when we were getting down and I had Perjah on my mind, but at the same time it let me know that I didn't have it in me to be faithful to her, and neither did she have it in her to be faithful to me. We weren't meant to be together. That's the honest to God truth. Our actions on both ends proved that.

I kneeled in front of her as she sat on the edge of the bed with her thighs slightly opened. I placed my hands on both of her knees. From this position, I could see my cum running out of her slit. It dripped onto the bed leaving a sticky trail. She smelled like sex and ass. Any other time it would've aroused me to go at her again, but I had to nip some shit in the bud. "You know what, Kalani? On my word, I ain't mad at you, shorty. You fucking Showbiz only confirmed the fact that you ain't ready to be my wife, especially if you laying there thinking about fucking my brother while we're doing our thing. It's something real foul about that, but like I said, I ain't tripping."

She shook her head. "Tristian, I swear I didn't mean to go down that road with him. It just happened. That doesn't mean that I'm not fit to be your wife or that we can't go the distance. I made one mistake. It'll never happen again. I'm sure that you haven't been perfect this whole time." She wiped tears from her cheeks.

"N'all, I haven't. In fact, I was thinking about somebody else while we were doing our thing too. It's obvious that neither of us is where we want to be. So, let's stop with the games. We deserve more than what we're giving each other. I don't fit you, shorty. You're free to take a shower. After that, I need you to get all your things from my crib and be on your way. No hard feelings." I stood up and her on the forehead.

She sat there for a while with her head down. "Tristian, if you break up with me, I can't be held responsible for the wrath that comes your way. I can't see you walking around knowing that you and I are no longer a part of one another. I just can't let that happen. I'm begging you not to do this to me." She said these words without looking up.

"Kalani, I love you. I always will, but I can't fuck you with on that level anymore. My heart ain't in it. Take a shower and move on with your life. Wish all the best."

"A'ight, Tristian." She nodded. "We'll do things your way. Okay."

Chapter 10

As soon as I walked into Brittany's hospital room, I could feel my heart pounding inside of my chest. Perjah took my hand and led me over to her bed. Brittany was sitting up with a big white teddy bear in her arms that I had sent up prior to my arrival this morning. She had a big smile on her face, showing both of her prominent dimples.

Perjah stepped in front of her bed. "Baby, I know that you've met him before without me being in the room, but now I'd like to properly introduce the both of you. Brittany, this is Tristian. And Tristian, this is my daughter Brittany."

I extended my hand and shook Brittany's smaller one, kissing the back of it. "How you doin', lil' mama? Long time no see."

"Fine, thank you. I can't wait to go home. I'm tired of being here. But my bear makes me feel safe." She hugged the big teddy bear. "I love the bear."

Man, my heart was beating so fast. She was so precious. I felt like I needed to protect her with everything in me. Anytime I looked into her pure eyes, I saw the shootout all over again. I wished I would've take those slugs for her so that she never had to.

I took her little hand into my own and held it. "Precious, when you get out of here, I'm going to take you shopping and buy you anything you want. Then, if it's okay with your mother, we'll go to Disney Land and have a wonderful time. Whatever it will take to prove to you that you are special, and you're a princess. You've been through a lot. From here on out, me and your mother are going to make sure that you are well-protected and taken care of. Okay?"

Her eyes lit up. She looked over to Perjah. "Mom, we're actually going to Disney Land? I've wanted to go there my entire life. That'll be so cool."

Perjah looked over to me and frowned. "Well, baby, we will discuss it further. First, we're going to concentrate on getting you healthy. That's the most important thing right now. Ain't that right, Tristian?" She gave me a look that said I needed to take it down a couple of notches.

I nodded. "Yes, that's right." I looked down at her and kissed her hand once again. "Is there anything that I can do for you right now, princess?"

She shrugged. "I don't know. I guess when it's time for me to get out of here, you can come and help my mommy. That way, no more bad guys can come and get me. I don't think you will anybody hurt me or my mommy. My dad is dead or else he would protect us." She poked out her bottom lip and lowered her head.

I sat on the edge of her bed and wrapped her up in my arms, hugging her for a spell. "Well, I'm here for you, Brittany. When you get out of this hospital, I'll be right there, front and center, ready to protect you from all the bad guys. I promise. I won't let you down."

"Thank you, Tristian. I believe you one hundred percent." She hugged me tighter and looked up at me with a smile on her precious face.

While I was holding her, an Arab nurse knocked on the door and stepped inside, followed by Brittany's grandmother. The older lady walked over to the bed and almost bumped me out of the way, so she could hug and kiss all over her.

Perjah grabbed my hand and led me into the hall. We walked out to the stairwell. She waited until the door closed before she tore into me. She waited until the door closed before she tore into me. She started poking me in the chest with her finger. I don't like people making promises to my daughter. You're out there in those streets every single day. Anything can happen to you at any given time. If something does happen to you, you won't be able to fulfill those promises. So, why bother making them?" She asked looking into my eyes.

"Perjah, I know how to survive out there. Everything that I've said to Brittany, I intend on living up to. I won't let her reach harm again. I will be here when she gets out of this place. And we're going to Disney Land as soon as you will allow it."

She shook her head. "Stop it, Tristian. I've been down this road before. I know that tomorrow isn't promised for you. Your life expectancy while being out in those New York streets is shorter than a candle wick. My daughter's father made her so many promises as well that he planned on keeping, but you know what? The life took him away from us. She was five years old. It's just me and her. Now this shooting happened and her you come. It's too much for a little girl. She's not ready for all of this change." She lowered her head.

I placed my fingers on her chin and made her look at me. "Perjah, y'all have been through a lot. I get it. But you do not have to do this alone. I won't let you. I'm not going anywhere."

"Tristian, you don't—"

I shook my head. "I do get it. You have to be this mother bear. You have to fight this world head on, alone, because you feel it's your only shot of not missing anything or allowing for anyone to hurt you or your baby again. I get it, but I will never allow for that to happen. I'd put my life on the line for that little girl in a heartbeat, and even though you and I are just getting to know each other, I would for you as well." I rubbed the side of her and laid my forehead against hers. She smelled of Prada Vanilla.

"It was my fault, Tristian. I should have never let her go with Flex that day, but she begged me. Begged me because she's been missing that male role model in her life ever since her father was murdered four years ago. I trusted him, and now my baby is in the hospital fighting for normalcy. I feel like the worst mother in the world." She laid her head on my chest and began to cry.

I closed my eyes as I held her. I was finally beginning to understand what was going on inside of her, but I wanted to explore the depths of her heart and mind. I wanted to get to know this woman as I've never known another. There was something special and extremely captivating about her. I needed her in my life. I couldn't explain why, but I felt a major pull to her.

"It wasn't your fault, Goddess. You did what you felt was right for her, and God knows this. The only way you can begin to heal is if you forgive yourself, so you can help in the process of Brittany healing. I'm not going anywhere. I promise you on my word as a man I'll stand by your side. We'll face every single battle together until she's one hundred percent. I got the both of you." I lifted her chin again, so I could look into her pretty brown eyes. "Do you believe me?"

She sighed. "I don't know what to believe just yet, Tristian. Actions speak so much louder than words. All I can agree to is us taking this day by day. I'd be a lie if I told you that this pending battle with her doesn't scare the daylights out of me. She has fifty thousand dollars in medical bills already and I'm praying that I can somehow afford her physical therapy because I don't receive any assistance from the state, so everything must come out of pocket. On top of that, my child will be released at the end of the week and I don't even have a place of residence for her. What kind of mother am I? I feel like such a loser." She exhaled and shook her head.

When me and my siblings turned eighteen we were finally able to have access to trust funds that my father had set up for us as infants in the amount of $500,00. I was only twenty-one years old, and in the three years that I'd had my trust fund, I'd only spent $100,000 of it. I still had $400,00 put up for when I graduated and stepped into the business world. After hearing some of the struggles that Perjah and Brittany were faced with, this money came to mind. There was no way that I could allow for them to struggle while I was in the picture. I was more of a man than that.

I held her pretty face in my hands. "Here's what we're going to do. First, I'ma take care of that lil' light fifty bands for her medical bills. Then, you're going to go online and see what kind of a crib you can find for the two of you. If you can't locate anything before she is released from here, you two will move in with me temporarily. If you don't trust me being there, then I'll stay in a hotel until you find a place. But I'm not going to let her be released into some hotel. That's not happening."

"Wait, Tristian. I can't let you do all of this. I don't know when I'll be able to pay you back, if ever. The job I work at now pays me less than four hundred a week. And now that Brittany will be home, I'll have to take more time off work. Our only income will come from the Social Security people, and I haven't even filed for that yet. So, you're looking at a life time before I'm able to pay you anything."

I kissed her forehead. "Perjah, it's good. I got this. Just let me handle my business. You and that baby don't owe me anything. It's for a chance to prove myself to the both of you. Can you render me that?"

She looked into my eyes and held her silence. Then she shook her head and closed her eyes for a brief period. "I've never depended on a man before. I've always been independent. I've worked so hard to instill in my daughter the importance of relying on herself. This is all going to be a struggle for me, so you'll have to be patient."

I brushed her hair out of her face and continued to hold her small face in my big hands. "You're still independent, Perjah, you just have a partner now that is going to ride beside you through it all. Any dreams that you have, I'll help you bring them into fruition. Just grant me this chance. It's all I ask."

134

She nodded. "And what do you want from me in return? Be honest too, because nobody does all these things for a person that they barely know for nothing. So, what gives?"

"I have no agenda. I just want to do what is right. Brittany, and even you, deserve exactly that."

* * *

Before I left the hospital, I allowed for them to swipe my Wells Fargo card, so they could take out Brittany's hospital fees. I wanted Perjah to hold her head high when she rolled Brittany out of Mount Sinai Hospital knowing that she no longer owed them one red cent. I could only imagine the burden being lifted from her shoulders, but we had so far to go. Deep down in my heart I was ready to go the distance with her and that baby girl. For the both of them, I felt like it was love at first sight for me. I wasn't about to abandon them under no circumstances.

On my way out of the hospital my mother hit my phone and texted me to meet at her home in Manhattan. It was unusual for her to leave me messages without stating her purpose, but I responded that I was on my way.

I got there, and she met me at her front door drying her hands on a yellow hand towel. She stepped on her tippy toes and kissed me on the cheek, stood back and slapped me across the face so hard that I wound up biting my tongue. I could taste the blood.

Afterward, she walked away from the door and I walked in behind her. "What was that for, ma?"

She stopped and turned around to face me. "Your father is dying, and you didn't tell me. On top of that, he's looking for a successor for his seat as the head of this family, and you've said nothing to me. Not a word. I have a mind to slap you again, Tristian. I swear that to Jehovah above."

I closed the door and ran my tongue into the corner of my mouth. I could feel where my skin split. A trickle of blood leaked out of it. "I didn't think you wanted to concern yourself with all of that drama, ma. Besides, Juanito already has that slot locked up. The last I checked he only needed five more million and that would be that. It's over with."

My mother stayed in a seven bedroom and five bath mansion on the upper part of Manhattan. She was 5'7" with long, curly black hair that flowed down her back. Her eyes wire pure brown. She weighed about a hundred and thirty pounds. She was a health-nut who did all forms of yoga and Pilates. She was originally from Chicago, Illinois. She'd moved to New York at the age of twelve and had been there ever since. She'd met my father when she was only fourteen years old. She had me at fifteen, and my sister at seventeen.

My mother ran five restaurants, two credit unions, and an Uber service out in New York. She was a well put together woman who was independent, and all about her paper. I looked up to her and didn't love anybody even a pinch as much as I loved her. She was the Queen of my heart. Always had been.

She picked up a glass of red wine from the glass table in her living room. The room had a crystal chandelier hanging from the ceiling. There was a painting on the wall of Michelle Obama, and another one of Harriet Tubman. My mother was a woman of courage and strength.

She took a sip out of her wine and smiled. "There is a chance for my son to be one of the most powerful men in all of New York and you didn't think that I would've loved to have that information. Are you freaking kidding me? That means that I won't have to work so hard." She pointed at me with her pinky finger. "I'll tell you what. You're not about to lose this to anyone of his other kids. You come from me which means that position is rightfully yours. I don't care how much money, Juanito had come up with already." She sat the glass on the table. "I can't believe I had to find out about all of this through Miguel. He's not even my son!" She balled her fists and took a deep breath.

I stepped further into the room and stood in front of her. "Why are you getting so worked up? I thought you'd prefer if I went to college and made something of myself. But it seems more like you'd rather for me to take over Pop's drug trade?"

She looked up at me. "Not only are you going to take over his seat, but you're going to sit there and rule from that position of power better than he ever could. One of the things you need to know is that I made your father the man that he is today. When I met him, he was nothing more than an illegal immigrant with some pretty light brown eyes. I got him plugged with my uncles in Chicago and they plugged him into the Underworld. Once in, your father used the knowledge that he'd learned from my people to incorporate it into the dope game. He took that knowledge back to Havana and linked up with a few power players from his island and the rest is history. But even so, from time to time I am the one that guides him. I am the one that irons out the wrinkles within his life. Let's take Senator Grant for example." She clapped her hands together and held her right one out.

A sharply dressed white man appeared out of the kitchen with a cigar in his hand. He stepped up to me with his hand out stretched. We shook. "How're doing Tristian? Your mother has told me so much about you."

I gave my mother a crazy look. "I wish I could say the same about you. May I ask who you are?"

My mother slid her arm around my shoulder. "This is Senator Jefferey Grant. He will become the next mayor of New York, and then governor. Through him, son, you will be able to create your own dynasty. He is already an animal in foreign affairs. Because of me, he and his friends here are on broad." She stepped forward and kissed his lips.

"Mmm, your mother is quite the woman, Tristian. I look forward to continuing my working closely with her and building a new relationship with you and your regime. It will be my honor."

"But first we'll have to get you elected which won't be that much work." She kissed his lips again. "When you become mayor, my son will be your number one priority, is that a fact?"

He kneeled and lowered his head. "That is a fact, my love." He kissed her hand and his eyes remained closed.

My mother looked over to me. "A man's place is on his knees." It's what my mother has always told me, and I couldn't agree more. "Get off your knee, Jefferey, and shoo. Leave me to talk things over with my son." She curled her upper lip and waved him away. After he left the living room, she motioned with her finger for me to follow her.

We stepped out of the back of the mansion where the pool was located. The sun shined off its light blue waters. There were two diving boards. One higher than the other. A bunch of lounge chairs were lined up to one side of the swimming pool. On the same sides were tables with an umbrella attached to them.

My mother walked in front of me. Her Prada sundress flowing in the wind along with her silky hair. I could smell her perfume. We made it into the well-furnished pool house and walked through the first room and into the back of it where she stood beside the fire place and pointed at the bed in the center of the room. Atop the bed were three big Burberry suitcases. The tops of them were opened, and all I could see was neatly stacked bundles of cash. They were face up. I could make out Benjamin's face.

"Your father said the first son to bring him fifteen million dollars would be the one he'd set upon his throne. Miguel said something about the Red Hook Houses." She waved that off. "They are infested and swarming with snitches. The federal government is looking to shut them down within the next five years. Who's ever in control of them from a street standpoint at that time will be thrown under the jail. That person will not be you. We are smarter than that. If Juanito wants to shoot for that challenge, then we'll let him. Maybe it'll keep him busy for a while." She laughed. "Now you are going to take this money to your father. If he asks how you obtained it, you point to your temple, and leave it at that. You tell him that a deal is a deal, and that the Red Hook Houses are a bad idea. Don't give him any more than that. He'll appreciate your moxy."

"Mama, I don't know what to say, other than what about Showbiz?"

She stepped forward and scratched affectionately behind my right ear. "Nothing changes for now, son. You'll still go to school. Those degrees are important. Mama still has a lot of kinks to work out, but the hard part is already done." She laughed. "It has never been a man's world, son. The world, since the beginning of time, has been ran by the woman. Men have never had enough comm_on sense to understand that. With everything that takes place in this world, I swear to you, on the love that I have for you as a mother, there has always been a woman behind it. Everything is by a woman, and men seek power to gain the love and admiration of a woman. Through you, son, your mother will remind the world what the muscle of a woman looks like. In the process, I will make you, my son, king of the world. I promise you this, or let death be my consequence." She stepped forward and wrapped her arms around me and kissed both of my cheeks. "Go, son. Go and handle your business."

Chapter 11

My father paced as the four Cuban women sent the bills of money through the four Microsoft Money Counting machines. He had an odd look on his face. His hands were clasped behind his back. I could tell he was in deep thought.

I was doped up off four Percocet thirties. My body felt so numb that I couldn't feel my hands that were placed on top of my knees. My eyes were low, and I was having a hard time keeping them open. I was thinking about Perjah and Brittany. It was a day before I was set to pick them up. Perjah had agreed to come and live at my crib because it was hard to locate one. I knew she was trying. She was still feeling some type of way about having to lean on me for support. I understood where she was coming from. Which was why I wanted to find out what her hopes and dreams were, so I could help her bring them into existence. She was supposed to be an independent woman. I was willing to invest into her in any way that I could for the long-term.

About an hour after I'd gotten to my father's mansion, Showbiz ran through the door of his den with two suitcases in his hands. He dropped them on the floor and rushed over to me with a mug on his face. "How did you do it, huh? How the fuck did you come up with fifteen million dollars before I could, Tristian?"

I stood up and stepped into his face, flaring my nostrils. With my index finger, I tapped my temple like my mother had told me to do.

He frowned. "What the fuck does that mean?" He snapped.

I did it again, and sat back on the couch, looking off into the distance. I was tired of all that tough acting shit. I didn't know how much more of it I could take before that real beast came out of me. Like I said before, I loved my brother with all my heart, but at the same time, I was still a man with pride.

"Yo, Pop, I'm smelling foul play here. There is no way that this bitch ass nigga could have come up with fifteen million dollars before me. I been pulling kick-doors and laying niggas down ever since you put forth this proposal. He ain't been on shit. The streets don't even know who this nigga is. Word is bond." He looked down on me with intense frustration.

My father walked over to him and pushed him to the couch. He spoke to him in Spanish. "Sit the fuck down, Juanito, and shut up. Have some decency about yourself. You're acting like an idiot." He-continued to pace in front of us.

I leaned over and placed my lips to Showbiz's ear. "Nigga, the next time you call me a bitch I'ma make you prove that shit. On my word, you starting to get real slippery with your tongue." I sat back on the couch after saying my peace.

Showbiz looked over to me and sucked his teeth. "On my word, nigga, I'd beat the fuck out of you, Kid. You're lucky you my brother. If you wasn't, I'd a slumped you a long time ago. That's on my mother."

My father stopped in mid-pace "I'm tired of you two always arguing and bickering. How will you carry on once I am gone?" He looked from me to Showbiz. "If both of you think that you are so tough, then go out the backyard and settle it once and for all. Only cowards speak so many words without putting actions behind them."

"What?" Showbiz jumped up. "Let's get it. I'll take him in the backyard and whoop his ass right now, Pop. You ain't saying nothing but a word." He kicked my Air Max. "Let's go, nigga. I'll fuck you up in front of Pop right now. Put these Harlem dukes on yo' ass."

I stood up and walked out the room, headed for the backyard. I was tired of Showbiz thinking it was sweet because he had a habit of killing women and kids. I felt like it was time that somebody whooped his ass anyway. That somebody should've been me.

When we got to the backyard, I took off my shirt and then my bulletproof vest. The sun shined down on my rock-hard abs, and chiseled chest. I rolled my head around on my shoulders and bounced on my tippy toes. I'd grew up fighting in Brooklyn. While going to James Madison High School I think I went a few months where I had to fight every single day, so it wasn't a thing for me. My only issue was that I honestly didn't want to fuck my brother up like I did other cats in the streets. I wanted to do just enough to get my point across.

My father picked up a chair and sat it right where he would have the best seat. His maid came out of the mansion and poured him a glass of pink lemonade. "What's taking you two so long? Fight already."

Showbiz took his pistols off his hip and laid on the table next to my father's glass. He stripped his shirt off and his bulletproof vest before walking into the grass with his guards up.

Miguel stepped out of the mansion along with three of my father's bodyguards. They were armed with cowboy hats on their heads and bushy mustaches. "Whoop his ass, Juanito. He thinks he's so tough." Miguel hollered.

I laughed and protected my chin with my right fist. "What's good, Showbiz?"

He bounced on his toes, and then rushed me swinging wildly. I could tell that he was going for the knockout punch. His first blow caught me in the side of the head. The second on my forearm. He was making guttural sounds that were off-putting. His technique was lazy, like his personality, impulsive.

I ducked one of his punches, saw an opening and jabbed him straight in the nose. I swung with a right hook and rocked him so hard that he staggered backward. But I wasn't done. I rushed him and caught him twice in the jaw with my left hand and hit him with another hook with my right.

He twisted in the air and fell on his side on the grass with blood dripping out of his mouth. I continued to dance on my toes. My adrenalin was pumping like crazy. I loved fighting. There was nothing like breaking another man down to size with your hands. It exerted dominance over him. It made me feel like a king.

Showbiz got to one knee and spat blood into the grass. He wiped

his mouth and looked up at me with hatred in his eyes. "That's how you wanna do it, Tristian? Huh?"

I kept dancing on my toes. Quiet niggas were the killers. The ones that ran their mouths to hype themselves up, in my opinion, were nothing more than cowards. So, I kept my comments to myself. Plus, I wasn't the type to use a lot of profane language in front of my father. I respected him more than that. He was my old man and I was his seed.

Showbiz stood all the way up, hollered, and rushed me at full speed with blood dripping from his chin. His arms were extended, I guessed ready to scoop me, but I had other plans in mind. I side stepped him, and as he flew past, I punched him three times in the jaw. Grabbed his ponytail and slung him to the ground. Before I could take a step back, Miguel rushed me with a baseball bat in his hand.

He whacked me across the back and I fell to my knees after crying out in pain. "Get the fuck off of my brother, nigger!" He tried to swing it again, when I swept his feet from under him and jumped up.

I threw my guards up, and Showbiz rushed me again, swinging wildly. I blocked all his attempts and uppercut him as hard as I could, knocking him clean out. Miguel rushed me with his head down. I scooped him in the air and slammed him on his back so hard that he bounced off the grass and landed on his side, groaning in pain.

I walked over to my vest, picked it up, then my shirt. I went over and looked at my father. "Now what, Pop?"

He handed me a glass of pink lemonade. "Now you sip until we get the sum of cash you brought to me. Job well done, son. I never doubted you for one second." He then went over to Showbiz and tapped him on the arm until he woke up.

An hour later, we were all sitting in the living room when one of the Cuban money counters stood up and announced to my father in Spanish that I handed him $15-million on the head.

My father nodded and turned to me. "Tristian, come here, Mijo."

Showbiz bounced to his feet, picked up his suitcases and stormed out of the den with Miguel walking behind him. Before Showbiz disappeared, he looked over his shoulder, into my eyes. "Long as I'm living, you will never be king, fuck nigga. This shit ain't over. On my mother, this shit is far from over."

Miguel held his ribs and shook his head. "We'll see you soon, brother."

"If you kids walk out of this den without me dismissing you, you'll be sorry. Now, come back here!" My father ordered. He started to cough uncontrollably. He took a handkerchief out of his pocket and wiped his mouth. I saw that there were speckles of blood on it.

"You think I'm finna sit back and watch you crown this fuck nigga? You out of your mind. You can give him your seat, but there can only be one king, and it's me. Let's go, Miguel." Showbiz waved my father off before they departed.

My father kneeled in front of me. "With power comes a lot of responsibility, Mijo. There is more to my throne than drugs. I want to take you on a trip with me, so I can show you some things. After you understand the roots of the Vegas, only then will you be fit to be king. You understand me?"

146

I pulled him up and wrapped my arms around him. "I do, Pop, and I always have. I love you, man."

"I love you too, son." He patted my back and took a step back, wiping his mouth. "Oh, and before I forget, take this money back to your mother and tell her I said stop being so power-hungry. I'll be dead soon. The Vegas will be hers through you." He smiled and shook his head. "I've always admired that woman. The love of my life, if I'm being quite honest." He said all these things in Spanish.

Chapter 12

Brittany was finally released from the hospital on a bright and sunny Friday afternoon. She was all smiles as I rolled her down the hallway of Mount Sinai hospital. She kept on looking up to me and cheesing. She hugged the big teddy bear tight in her little arms. "I can' believe I'm getting out of here, mama. It feels like I've be n in here for forever."

Perjah leaned down and kissed her on the cheek. "But you haven't, baby. You're finally out of this place. I'm so happy you made it!"

Brittany closed her eyes and smiled, accepting the kiss. "And are we going to Disney Land right away, Tristian. That would be so cool! The ultimate celebration."

I laughed and rubbed her soft cheek. "Soon Princess. I promise you that'll be real soon."

Perjah rolled her up to my truck while I opened the back door. Then, I went around, picked her up and carried her to the backseat before strapping a seatbelt across her. "You good, lil' mama?" I asked, kissing her cheek.

She shook her head and reached for the big, white teddy bear. "I need my bear, mama. Can you hand it to me?" she cried.

Perjah grabbed the bear out of the wheelchair and handed it to her with a worried expression on her face. I was thinking that the bear had become more of a sensory object for Brittany. I noticed it when I'd first wheeled her out of the hospital with how she'd had her arms around it and to it for dear life. Though the hospital had been a place of boredom for her, it was still something like a safe haven. Now that she was leaving, the reality of what she'd been through was setting in. I worried that she was suffering from a minor case of traumatic stress disorder.

"It's okay, baby girl. We're here. I'm not about to let nothing happen to you. I promise."

She looked up at me and hugged the bear to her chest. With her right hand, she reached for a hug. "Don't let nobody shoot me, Trista. It hurt me so bad the last time."

Damn. I felt sick at hearing that. My entire face flushed. I got a big lump in my throat and I felt like shedding tears. I tossed my keys to Perjah. "Go ahead and roll the whip. I'ma stay back here with her to make sure that she's okay. I ain't about to let nothing happen to this angel."

Perjah nodded and looked at Brittany. "Baby, would you prefer if he stayed back there with you while I drove to our new place? He can be your protector."

Brittany hugged me tighter. "Yes, mama. I need him, too."

Perjah jumped in the front seat and pulled away from the hospital. As it disappeared in the rearview mirror, I noticed that Brittany's eyes had gotten bigger and bigger. When it was no longer in sight, she began to shake with sweat pouring down the side of her forehead, even though the air conditioner was on blast.

I interlocked our fingers and kissed the back of her hand. "It's okay, baby. I'm right here with you." I was on my knee alongside her.

Perjah, from time to time, would look over her shoulder or watch us from the rearview mirror. Her eyes were often watery. I could tell that she was going through an emotional battle seeing her daughter in that state. I understood that I needed to be there for her as much as I possibly could, emotionally. After all, no matter how tough she was, she was only human.

* * *

That night, after Perjah gave Brittany a nice bath in the big tub and took a shower herself, they filed into the dining room where I whipped them up some of my mother's infamous Chicago Fried Chicken. I dipped every piece in a sweet, barbecue sauce from my mother's recipe, cut up some potatoes and turned them into French fries, and served a nice bowl of baked macaroni and cheese as a side. My mother had made me a German Chocolate cake and I was glad that she had because I planned on sharing it with them. We'd top it off with vanilla ice cream, when I found out this night that it was Brittany and Perjah's favorite flavor.

We held hands and said grace around our food before diving in like hungry savages. Brittany drank fruit punch juice, and Perjah and I had red wine. During the dinner the only thing Brittany kept talking about was Disney Land. She couldn't wait to go and prayed that we could go before the summer ended. She wanted to see the Black Panther set up they had added to the theme park. She couldn't believe that there were Black superheroes.

After dinner, she rolled into the living room, and we all sat and watched the Black Panther movie until she fell asleep. I picked her up and carried her into the spare bedroom that Perjah and I set up for her. We kneeled together and prayed over her before taking turns, kissing her on the forehead and leaving the room with the door slightly opened and her Frozen night light on.

Perjah stepped into the living room and ran her fingers through her hair. She exhaled loudly and placed her hands on her lower back, mumbling to herself.

I grabbed the remote and muted the television. "What's the matter, Perjah? Talk to me."

She sat on the couch and looked off into the distance. "I don't

think I'm strong enough for this, Tristian. I see how shaken up and damaged my little girl is, and it's killing me. The realization that she might be paralyzed for the rest of her life had just hit me. What am I going to do? How will I support her? I can't expect you to take care of us forever." She laid her face into her open hands.

I slid next to her on the couch and rubbed her back. "She gon' get better, Perjah. You have to have faith in that. And as far as you having to depend on me to survive until she gets better, I'm gon' make sure that you can. I got the both of you. I'll keep telling you this until you believe it for yourself. I got you. Please know that. I ain't going nowhere."

She lifted her hands from pretty face. Tears ran down her cheeks. "Why is that so hard for me to believe, Tristian? I mean, I want to believe it. Due to the position that me and my daughter are in, I have to believe it. But what's stopping you from becoming overwhelmed by it all? Who's to say that a year from now, or a month, you won't wake up and be over the both of us?"

I kneeled in front of her and brushed her hair out of her face. I'd somehow grown accustomed to doing that. I loved her long, flowing pretty hair. It made her look like a Queen to me. "I'm the one that says nothing like that will ever happen, and it won't. I'm the most loyal person you'll ever meet. Now, I've been fighting to be apart Brittany's life ever since the day we were shot. Now that you've granted me the opportunity to be here, I will never give you a reason to regret it. I need the both of you, Perjah, just as much as you guys need me. I'm here, baby, and I'm not goin' anywhere."

Snot ran out of her nose. I wiped it away and onto the leg of my pants. She blinked more tears, looking me over. She shook her head and exhaled. "I just don't understand why God sent you to me, but I am thankful for you, Tristian. What the devil meant for bad, God meant for good." She ran her hand over the top of my deep waves and smiled. "Would you be willing to kiss the lips of a crying woman?"

I continued to look deep into her penetrating eyes. "You better believe it."

I leaned in and pecked her real soft on the lips at first. She closed her eyes and kissed me back. I sucked her bottom lip into my mouth and cherished the taste of it. It was juicy and hot.

She moaned into my mouth, "I'm so thankful for you, Tristian. You have no idea."

I continued to suck all over her thick lips. I held her waist and trailed my hand downward, rubbing all over her ample backside. It was nice and round. Soft, yet firm. I felt like I was rubbing on a girl's booty for the first time. Butterflies were in my stomach. I felt giddy and excited. This was Perjah, and she was doing something to me that had never been done before. I could tell that this would be the kiss that would leave me addicted to her. "I'll never leave your side, Perjah. I promise you, baby. You have no idea how much your presence means to me."

I trailed my kisses down to her neck and bit into it. She moaned at the top of her lungs and stepped forward into me. I sucked all over her neck and on to the middle of her chest. I pushed her up against the wall and sucked her round nipples through the Top Shop blouse that she was wearing. Her nipples were hard in my mouth.

She raised the shirt over her head and threw it to the carpet. Then, she placed her right hand on my neck, guiding me back to her breasts. "Go ahead, Tristian. Make me believe you. Heal me, and in turn I'll heal you too."

I squeezed her breasts together and groaned deep within my throat. I sucked first her left erect nipple into my mouth and pulled on it. It popped out of my lips and stood up like a wet Hershey kiss. Her nipples were huge. The areola was circular like a fifty-cent piece. I went back and forth from one unto the other. I wondered if she could see the empty hole inside of me. I wondered if she could tell that I felt alone in life. That I needed a reason to breathe. I yearned to have someone to render unconditional love to me so that I, in turn, could do the same for her. I was silently broken. I couldn't quite say what I wanted out of life with certainty, especially since my father was close to giving me his throne. I didn't know if I was ready, or if I wanted it to begin with. The only thing I knew in that moment was that I needed Perjah. I needed her more than I had ever needed a woman before in my life, and that terrified me because I was led to believe that men never needed women in that context. That they were supposed to be at a man's disposal and nothing more. My whole life I'd never witnessed a relationship between a man and woman that worked.

Perjah started to unbuckle my Gucci belt before unbuttoning the pants and pulling them down my thighs. I stepped out of them. She kissed my lips and slid her tongue into my mouth. "I need you to make love to me, Tristian. I'm not asking you to screw me like you've probably done a lot of women in the past. I need to feel you healing me. I'm broken right now. Can you do that?" She looked into my eyes, sucking on her bottom lip.

I nodded and picked her up. She wrapped her legs around my waist and laid her head on my shoulder as I carried her into my bedroom and stopped with her back against the wall. I sucked her lips into my mouth once again. We tongued each other down, breathing heavily. The taste of her was enough to send shivers up and down my spine. I laid her in the middle of the bed and pulled her pants from her body.

She opened her legs wide, causing the red laced panties she wore to become trapped in between her kitty lips. I could make out a hint of each lip that separated the cloth. It looked better to me than the $15-

million my mother had accrued for me. I crawled across the bed and placed my nose right on the crotch and inhaled her lovely scent. She smiled like a woman in deed.

I kissed her lips through the material and licked up and down the seat of her panties.

She moaned and opened her legs wider. "Oooh, it's been so long, Tristian. It's been so, so long." She pulled the panties to the side, exposing her meaty gap her juices leaked out of her body.

I leaned forward and slurped them into my mouth. I thank God for this blessing because He specially crafted her for me. I took pleasure in swallowing her essence. I pulled her panties all the way to the side and kept it there with my thumb as I went to work on her. "It's okay, Perjah. It's okay. I got you. I got you, ma," I said between slurps. I needed her to know that I was there. That I had her. That when it came down to it she could depend on me. She was so bad that I wanted to rush to and get on top of her and do my thing. I needed to see how she felt on the inside. I wanted to finally put a conclusion to the wonder I had going on inside of my brain about her internal treasures. But the common sense within me said that I should take it slow. That I should treasure the moment with her and make it all about her. So that's what I intended on doing.

She bucked against me, bit into her bottom lip, then pushed my head away from her kitty. "Wait, Tristian. I don't know if this is right. I mean we haven't even established if you and I are going to be together just yet. I don't want to make any crazy decisions just because of my vulnerable state right now.

I'm not that kind of woman." She scooted back and tried to sit up on her elbows.

I continued to kiss her inner thighs, sucking the juices from them. Her kitty was leaking. I was so hard that my piece was jumping. I could feel my penis head throbbing like a heart. I needed her so bad. I sat back on my haunches and looked down at her after wiping my mouth with the back of my hand. She looked so damn fine. All caramel and glistening. She had a few stretch marks that decorated her stomach, an outie belly button, and light freckles on her breasts. I found her so sexy and appealing. The animal in me wanted her. I was mentally crying out for her. I shook my head. "Perjah, we ain't gotta do this then. If you'll let me, I'll hold you all night. I'll do whatever you need me to."

She sat up and put her back against the headboard. I was sick when she closed her thighs and took the sight of her meaty treasures away from me. I could still smell her on my top lip. Her essence was all over my tongue. My penis was jumping like crazy.

She ran her fingers through her hair and exhaled. "What are we going to do after this? Are we going to try and be together, or will this just be a one-night stand that will mean absolutely nothing in the morning? I need to know what you're thinking before I do something that I've never done before and be honest with me."

I wanted some of her body so bad. Because she was so fine to me I was willing to say anything to break the barriers of her sex lips. I'd never seen a sista so righteous to my eyes. But then there was apart a part of me that couldn't lie to her. I had to tell her exactly what I was thinking and feeling. I felt she deserved the truth. Not only that, but I also wanted to start this relationship with her on a righteous level without all the lies and games. I'd had enough of that with Kalani. I was a grown man with the weight of the world on my shoulders.

"I know it is still pretty premature for me to be talking like this, but I'm willing to go out on a limb. I like you. I already love Brittany and I know that will never change. I feel like I can be a benefit to the both of you, and vice-versa. Now, it's like I said, I'll do anything that you want me to do tonight, but if it was up to me, I'd make love to you until the sun came up because my body is calling for you."

She got on her knees and walked across the bed until her nose was against mine. She looked into my eyes. "I don't know why, Tristian, but I trust you. I want you just as bad as you want me. As far as everything else goes, I'd like to work on that starting first thing in the morning." She smiled and sucked my lips into her mouth. She wrapped her arm around my neck, pulled me down on top of her, opening her thick thighs wide.

I pulled her panties off her, stripped down until I was as naked as the day I came into the world, and got between her thighs. "Are you sure this is what you want, because we don't have to do this." I kissed her lip, and sucked on the bottom one, pulling it away from the other one.

"I don't want to think right now, Tristian. I just want you to make love to me. I need to be in a faraway land for just a little while. In the morning, I'll face my responsibilities. But not tonight. I want you." She reached between us, grabbed a hold of my piece and placed it on her leaking hole. Spread her lips and guided me in. "Uh. Okay, now do you, but take it slow." She wrapped her arms around my neck and licked my lips.

I humped forward and entered her warmth. It felt like a silk fire place. Her opening was so tight that it took me a little work to get into her. It felt so good that my eyes rolled into the back of my head. I moaned and lunged forward. "It's good, Perjah. It's good, ma."

She arched her back and opened her legs wider. "Take. Me. Away, Tristian. Take. Me. Away. I don't. Want. To. Be. Here. Right. Now." She moaned, sucking all over my lips and running hands down my muscular back. I felt her nails penetrating me a few times.

I cocked my back and slid deeper and deeper into her wetness. The sounds that came out of her mouth were driving me crazy. More than once I wanted to turn into a savage and kill that good gushy, but I knew I had to stay the course. I didn't want to scare her away or break our understanding. It wasn't about me, it was about her, and me being in her oasis. The connection was everything for me. I knew that it was the beginning of a beautiful relationship between her and myself.

Perjah arched her back and moaned into my mouth. "It's so good, Tristian. It's so good. You're hitting all my spots. Uhh! Yes. You're hitting my spots." She dug her nails into my lower waist. "You can go a lil' faster. It's okay. Just a little bit. Yes. Yes!" She hugged me to her warm body.

I followed her command and sped up just enough. My waist went in circles every time I lunged forward. I went as deep into her as I could reach. Her heat was intense. The rivers of her juices leaked like lava, only stickier. I loved every stroke of her. I was sure that the sounds I was making told her just that. I reached between us, rubbing her clit with my thumb before pinching it.

Her nails dug into my back. She bit my neck and screamed. "Uh! Tristian! Thank you, baby! Ooh!" She wrapped her legs around me and started to shake uncontrollably.

My thumb continued to work vigorously on her clit. My pole slid in and out of her box deeper and deeper. I pulled all the way back and slammed home. My body tensed before the euphoric feeling took over me and sent me over the edge.

"Ugh. Ugh. Damn, Perjah." I started to cum over and over again, deep within her channel.

She ran her hands all over my chest and licked her lips real sexy like. She pulled me back on top of her so that we were chest to chest. "Okay, Tristian. Now, take it nice and slow."

I hugged her to my body, sucked her neck and slowly stroked her for the rest of the night until we eventually passed out some time after five in the morning. The last thing I remembered was having a smile on my face as I fell beside her, smelling like strong sex.

Chapter 13

Me, Perjah and Brittany got closer and closer over the next four weeks. We spent them cooped up in the house where we took turns getting to know one another. I found out that Perjah's birthday was on the twenty-seventh of April just like mine. That we were born in the same hospital, and had gone to the same high school, though she was a senior while I was still in the ninth grade. I found out her favorite foods and movies, and we even ordered some of them while we ate pizza in front of my big smart screen television. She was extremely helpful with my studies online, and I'd also found out that she had been one credit away from receiving her business degree. I wanted to help her obtain it. I knew that with that degree in her hands that the sky was the limit for her and her daughter.

Kalani, stopped by once and I'd met up with her on the porch. I wasn't really trying to give her no word play. Every time she came through she'd start out like everything was cool, but five minutes into our conversation she'd find a way to bring some form of drama into it. I was over all of that and told her to never come back unless she called and got my permission. Once again, she promised me that I'd be sorry for how I was doing her, even though I felt I was being as respectful as possible.

The last time Kalani had come through, Perjah waited until I closed the door before she asked me what was good with Kalani and myself, and I told her what it was. That she and I had, at one point in time, had been together, but had decided to slow things down until we were able to accomplish some of our goals in life. That even though we had slowed things down that we were still sleeping together on a weekly basis, but there weren't any emotions involved. At least not on my part. That during the time we had to focus on the bigger picture of things, she'd admitted to sleeping I with my brother. After I found that out, I'd cut her off for good.

Perjah sighed as she sat on the couch beside me and interlocked our fingers. "We each have a past so I'm not going to hold anything that you have done before me against you. That isn't fair. But I will say this. Every time a woman lies down with a man, there are always emotions involved. If that woman is continuing to come around looking for you, she still cares and will not step aside without a fight, Tristian. I care about you, and I think we can build something strong, but I cannot be involved in a love triangle. I have a special needs daughter and a plate full of burdens. I'm asking you to nip things in the bud with her, so we can be happy together. Please."

I understood where she was coming from. I appreciated the way she came at the situation and I had it on my mind to get an understanding with Kalani as soon as I possibly could.

My father got, Jefferey Grant's campaign up and running with a vengeance. It seemed in a months' time, Senator Grant ads were all on buses and bus benches, and he was all over the news. There were billboards of him all over the city. It seemed like you couldn't go a day without seeing an interview with him. He was killing it in the polls. Especially after sex allegations came against the current mayor of the city. Grant went ahead in the polls by a whopping thirty points. He was cruising his way to a victory and I'd never seen my father happier in my life.

The day that Senator Grant had won the election, my father called me into his study and we'd watched it all on his big screen. After the final results were announced, he stood up and shook my hand. "Mijo, you have no idea what this means for the family. I need you more than ever. I am proud of you, kid, and I will be at your graduation next week. I can't wait to see you walk across that stage. After you do, we're taking a trip to Havana. I want to introduce you to some very important people." He started to cough into his handkerchief. When he took it away, he looked down at the blood speckled across it.

I grew worried about his health. "Pop, how long do you have now?" I swallowed and looked him over. He looked as if he'd lost another twenty pounds. I could see the bones in his face more prominently now. He'd once been a man full of muscles like me. I didn't know what losing my father looked like. I feared it with every fiber of my being.

He started to cough some more before placing his hand on my shoulder. "Just enough time to crown you as my successor. No matter what happens to me, you can always trust Shapiro. He is my right hand, son. He's never gotten over on me. I believe that he will guide you in the ways of the Vegas. I've taken good care of him, son. His heart is pure as can be." He broke into a fit of coughs.

I patted him on the back, even though it didn't help one bit. I wanted to hug my old man, but I knew he wasn't the overly affectionate type. I then kissed him on the cheek though. "I love you, Pop, with my whole heart. I'll be the man that you expect for me to be. You have my word on that."

Shapiro knocked on the door to the office and stepped inside. He stopped in place. "Am I interrupting anything here?" He looked directly to my old man.

My father coughed into his handkerchief and waved his hand. He shook his head. "No, what's up, Shapiro?"

"Boss, they want you in the Hamptons in the next hour to congratulate Senator Grant on a job well done. But before you attend that ceremony, I have more pressing matters."

My father stepped past me and stopped in front of him. "Go ahead."

"It's Bruno Gomez, sir. He's been released on five million dollars' bond and has fled to Cuba. He's saying that your family has attacked his, and he's waging war on the Vegas. He's assembling the troops back in Havana. This could cost us a lot of money." Shapiro sighed.

My father sat on the edge of his desk and lowered his head in deep thought. "I have no idea what he's talking about. Maybe he's aware that Senator Grant is on the Vegas payroll and he's jealous."

Shapiro shook his head. "According to sources in his camp, the Vegas are responsible for the deaths of his two sons, Chulo and Wisin. And, his granddaughter, Mardi. Do you know anything about this?" he asked my father.

My father rubbed his chin and shook his head. "Not the slightest. What about you, Mijo?"

I exhaled and blew air through my teeth. "Yeah. Pop. The order came down from Juanito. I wasn't there when the sons were killed but I am sure that he killed Mardi in cold blood."

My father broke into a fit of coughs and bent over. "That fucking Juanito. He never listens. He's just costed this family millions of dollars. A war with the Gomez's is the last thing we need. How in the fuck did he get out of jail anyway? I thought he was done." My father wipe his mouth and sat behind his desk.

Shapiro shrugged. "Politics. You know it goes in Washington. He's probably greased a few palms over at the agency. Either way, he's out, he's fled, and we can expect an attack some time very soon. Bruno is vicious. One of the dirtiest sons of bitches I've ever known."

My father shook his head. "Congratulations, Mijo, your reign kicks off with a war that can be life altering for the Vegas. I have full confidence in you. Shapiro, from here on out, you look at Tristian as you would me. He's a month away from being King." My father sat back in his chair and looked me over with pride in his eyes.

Shapiro stepped in front of me and shook my hand. "I'm proud of you, kid. It sucks that there won't be an easier transition for you, but you'll learn that in this life you have to expect the unexpected. Now let me bring you up to speed on a few things."

He took the next hour to break down the psyche of Bruno Gomez. It was my understanding that the man was calculating and cold hearted. He had no regard for women or children. He believed in torture and public humiliation. The Gomez's had gained power behind their name by raiding villages and taking over sugar cane field that they'd converted into cocaine and poppy fields. They made their money strictly from their drug trade. Behind Bruno was a deadly cartel of animals that called themselves the Black Knights. According to Shapiro, they were a pyramid of assassins in which Bruno sat at the top of. He called all the shots and funded the organization.

Shapiro assured me that my family was not to be taken lightly. My father had cold hearted savages in the island of Cuba and in New York. Savages that killed at the drop of a hat. They called themselves the Demons. My father made sure that all the families kept food on the table and clothes on their backs. He paid them handsomely and made sure they were protected politically. Most had families that sought asylum right here in the States. Because of my old man, they were protected from ICE. There was never a threat of deportation or arrest. The Demons lived on my father's word, and now that I was taking over his throne, they would live by mine.

Chapter 14

It was a long drive back to my brownstone in Brooklyn. I had so many things going through my mind that I could barely think straight. My head was pounding worse than ever. My stomach was in knots. On top of that, I was feening for my pills. I needed them just to be able to cope. I could tell that my father was on his way out of the game. Within ever cough was a drop of blood. He lost weight rapidly, and he couldn't say more than a sentence without it seeming as if he was losing his breath. It scared me to image him not being around, but I knew I had to man up because my duties as the head of the family were vastly approaching. I only had the slightest idea of what was to be expected.

In conjunction to all of that, I'd fall in love with Brittany. I wanted to be a part of her life for the rest of mine. I wanted to be there when she recovered and got back to full strength. I believed in her and knew that she needed me to remain beside her, holding her hand every step of the way while Perjah took a hold of her other hand and supported her from that side.

Speaking of Perjah, I cared about her already. I know that it might sound crazy, but I could see longevity in her eyes. I felt I could be with her wholeheartedly and help her to become the best version of herself. She seemed like the type of female that would stand by a man against all odds. She'd been through a lot, and I could tell that she was ready for something different. She often felt lost and without direction. I got the impression that she was used to doing things on her own. Figuring out the impossible.

This new turn of events with me standing beside her reassuring her that she could depend on me the long-haul was going to be difficult for her to accept and get used to it. I wasn't going nowhere. I was locked in and had already decided that I was going to be her ride or die man with no strings attached.

Right before I pulled up to my crib it started to rain like crazy. Big bolts of lightning flashed across the sky before striking and hitting a light pole about a block down. The street light zapped off and like thirty seconds later flipped back on. I sat there in my truck for about ten minutes with my stomach cramping. I slid two fingers under my vest and pressed in my abdomen again and again to gain some sense of relief, but it didn't happen.

My mother sent me a text saying that she needed to meet with me. That it was important. I texted her that it was storming like crazy outside and I'd see her after my class the next day. Her response was to say that Senator Grant was about to change our lives. I texted back that I hoped so, and I'd see her tomorrow.

I flipped the hood up on my Marc Jacobs jacket, took the key out of the ignition, grabbed my pistol, and ran out into the rain just as lighting flashed across the sky. I took the steps to my brownstone two at a time. I got to the door and opened it before rushing inside, shaking the rain off me.

For some reason my crib was extremely dark this night. There were no lights on in the house and that struck me as odd. I remembered wondering if Perjah and Brittany had stepped out, but then decided against it because Perjah's Plymouth Neon was parked in front of the crib. I turned the light on in the front room.

"Perjah! Perjah, ma, are you here?" I hollered, walking into my living room, flipping the lights on. I damn near jumped out of my skin when the lights revealed Showbiz sitting at my living room table with two guns on top of it. He had a frown on his face and an ounce of heroin on a plate in front of him.

He sucked his teeth and looked up at me with his upper lip curled. "So, you think you're about to steal my birth right, huh, Tristian?" He leaned down tooted a line of the China White heroin. "Nigga, over my dead body." He grabbed the guns off the table and scooted back in his chair. The legs of the chair scraped against the hardwood floors. He stood up with the guns in his hand.

I cocked my .40 Glock and raised it, aiming it directly at his head. "Say, Kid, you real high right now. I don't know how the fuck you got in my crib, but I'ma give you a few seconds to be on your way, or you be one dead brother. That's my word, kid."

"You ain't fit for the throne, Tristian. You ain't got that killer shit in you like I do. Nah'mean?" He pulled on his nose and smiled crookedly.

"Yo, I'm already King. That throne is mine. If I gotta take yo' head off to cement that, then so be it. You got thirty seconds to get the fuck out of my house. One. Two. Three—"

"Ahh!" There was a loud, piercing scream that came from downstairs. It sounded like a female.

Showbiz shook his head. "Tristian, Tristian, Tristian. I don't give a fuck about what Pops said. Nigga, as long as I'm living, you'll never be king of the Vegas. That's my muthafucking birth right and ain't nobody don't take that from me." He raised both guns and aimed them at me, cocking the hammers. "Let's get it, bitch nigga."

There was another piercing scream. This time it caused my heart to skip a beat. It was either Perjah or Brittany. It couldn't have been anybody else.

"In order to be king, Tristian, your heart has to be cold. You gotta stay one step ahead of your enemies at all times." He laughed. "I got bitches downstairs. I think it's only fitting we play a lil' game. You know, make shit interesting before I put these slugs in your face." He wiped his nose with the back of his hand and never took his eyes off me.

I bit into my lip and placed my finger around the trigger, ready to blat his ass. "That's the one thing about you, Showbiz. You love preying on the weak. Now yo' punk ass solely targeting women?"

He scoffed and walked backward down the hall-way. "Let's go, Tristian. Let's join the party so you can see what it is." He slowly backed down the hall with his eyes and guns pinned on me.

I kept my pistol on him, as we made our way down the long hallway and to the backdoor that led into the basement. I watched him open it and slip out. I followed close behind, praying that I wasn't about to find either Perjah or Brittany dead. I knew that Showbiz ain't have any problems killing a female, or a child. He was rotten like that.

We wound up walking all the way into the basement. It was illuminated by a red light because from time to time I liked to go down there and smoke a few blunts to take the edge off. When I stepped off the last stair I nearly freaked out from what I saw. Right there in the middle of the basement stood Miguel. He had a .357 Magnum in his hand, and it was aimed at Perjah's temple. She was on her knees with her back facing me. Beside her was Brittany. She was laid on her back with her arms stretched over her head sobbing.

Miguel had his Timb on her back. "'Bout time yo' bitch ass showed up, Tristian. Yo, Showbiz, word to my mother, you gotta let me fuck this lil' thick bitch right here. I can tell that she got a shot on her." He laughed and pressed e barrel more firmly to the back of her head.

I was ready to panic. Instead of having my gun aimed at Showbiz, now it was on Miguel. "What the fuck y'all on, bruh? They ain't got nothing to do with this."

Showbiz lowered his pistol walked in front of Perjah. "Nigga, they got everything to do with this." He pointed to his right and for the first time I noticed that there was another person in the basement off in the distance. I could see bare feet. Somebody was laying around them.

I scrunched my face. "Who's that, Showbiz? Damn."

"I told you there could be no loose ends. That ain't how the game go, Tristian. That bitch had to go." He stepped forward and grabbed a handful of Perjah's hair, yanking her head backward. She yelped in pain. "Now this bitch gotta go too." He pointed both guns at her.

I could hear her say, "He killed my niece, Tristian. He killed her for no reason. She was only fifteen." Perjah cried.

I couldn't for the life of me understand how she could be focused on that dilemma when he had two guns in her face, until I took a step to my right and saw that her eyes were duct taped, so she couldn't have known.

"What's it gon' be, Tristian, because this bitch's brother killed my lil' nigga. Somebody gotta pay for his sins. Flex's blood wasn't enough. On top of that, nigga you fucked up when you put yo' hands on me in front of Pops. I can't take that L. Its either gon' be you or this bitch. Unless you want me to stank this lame duck on the concrete. I mean, she half dead anyway." He snickered.

I looked from Miguel to him, then down to Perjah and then Brittany. The pool of blood from Perjah's niece had spread into the portion of the basement that we were in.

"I ain't playing, Tristian, you better make up your mind." Showbiz warned, cocking his hammers.

Miguel lowered his eyes. "Matter of fact, bitch, drop that pistol before I whack shorty ass. It ain't sweet, drop that muthafucka right now."

I raised my hands. "A'ight, bruh. Just calm yo ass down." I set the pistol on the floor on the side of me and placed my hands back at shoulder level. "Yo, you can let them go, Showbiz, and smoke me. They ain't got shit to do with this. You smoke me, you'll get your revenge and reclaim your birth right. All I ask is that you let them go and live their lives without having to worry about you niggas attacking them in the future."

Showbiz shook his head. "I told you, Miguel. This nigga is too soft to be king. He ready to die for these hoes and he don't even really know 'em. Pops gotta be the stupidest nigga in the world to think this nigga can take over the Vegas."

Miguel laughed. "We smoke him and these hoes. What you think?" He moved Showbiz out of the way before aiming his gun down at Perjah.

I don't know what came over me but as soon as I saw him move Showbiz out of the way, I kneeled and picked up my .40 off the ground, aimed and fired four shots into his chest. *Boom. Boom. Boom. Boom.* He flew backward into Showbiz before sliding down his body with blood leaking out of him.

Brittany screamed and covered her head with her hands. I could hear her sobbing more loudly now.

Perjah fell to her side and wiggling around on the floor like a fish out of water. "What happened? What happened? Oh, Lord, please tell me my baby is alright!" she cried.

Showbiz kneeled and wrapped his arm around her neck. He placed the gun to her temple. "I'll kill this bitch, Tristian. You know I will. Drop that gun, nigga. Drop that gun or on my mother in Cuba this bitch is dead." He promised.

The tape had somehow fallen from Perjah's eyes when he'd snatched her up. Tears ran down her cheeks. "Please, Tristian. Please, don't let him kill me."

I bit into my lower lip with my gun aimed at Showbiz. I was caught in a dilemma. If I put the pistol on the ground, there was a ninety percent chance that he was going to kill everybody in that basement. Especially after I hit up Miguel.

On the other hand, I knew that Showbiz was also kamikaze. If he felt like he couldn't get out of a situation, he would go all out. It was in his nature. I ran the risk of him killing Perjah and then having a not so glorious shootout. I didn't know what to do. I had the ups on him. I could simply kill him, and he'd probably kill her, but I'd still be alive along with Brittany.

I looked down at her as she sobbed on the ground. She started to shake uncontrollably. Out of instinct, I dropped the gun and knelt beside her, ready to assist her when all hell broke loose.

Boom. Boom. Boom.

To Be Continued...
King of New York 2
Coming Soon

Submission Guideline.

Submit the first three chapters of your completed manuscript to ldpsubmissions@gmail.com, subject line: Your book's title. The manuscript must be in a .doc file and sent as an attachment. Document should be in Times New Roman, double spaced and in size 12 font. Also, provide your synopsis and full contact information. If sending multiple submissions, they must each be in a separate email.

Have a story but no way to send it electronically? You can still submit to LDP/Ca$h Presents. Send in the first three chapters, written or typed, of your completed manuscript to:

LDP: Submissions Dept
Po Box 870494
Mesquite, Tx 75187

DO NOT send original manuscript. Must be a duplicate.

Provide your synopsis and a cover letter containing your full contact information.

Thanks for considering LDP and Ca$h Presents.

<u>Coming Soon from Lock Down Publications/Ca$h Presents</u>

BOW DOWN TO MY GANGSTA

By **Ca$h**

TORN BETWEEN TWO

By **Coffee**

BLOOD STAINS OF A SHOTTA **III**

By **Jamaica**

WHEN THE STREETS CLAP BACK **III**

By **Jibril Williams**

STEADY MOBBIN

By **Marcellus Allen**

BLOOD OF A BOSS **V**

By **Askari**

LOYAL TO THE GAME **IV**

By **T.J. & Jelissa**

A DOPEBOY'S PRAYER **II**

By **Eddie "Wolf" Lee**

IF LOVING YOU IS WRONG… **III**

LOVE ME EVEN WHEN IT HURTS

By **Jelissa**

TRUE SAVAGE **V**

By **Chris Green**

TRAPHOUSE KING **III**

By **Hood Rich**

BLAST FOR ME **III**

By **Ghost**

ADDICTIED TO THE DRAMA **III**

By **Jamila Mathis**

LIPSTICK KILLAH **III**

CRIME OF PASSION **II**

By **Mimi**

WHAT BAD BITCHES DO **III**

THE BOSS MAN'S DAUGHTERS **V**

By **Aryanna**

THE COST OF LOYALTY **II**

By **Kweli**

SHE FELL IN LOVE WITH A REAL ONE **II**

By **Tamara Butler**

LOVE SHOULDN'T HURT **II**

By **Meesha**

CORRUPTED BY A GANGSTA **III**

By **Destiny Skai**

A GANGSTER'S CODE II

By **J-Blunt**

KING OF NEW YORK II

By **T.J. Edwards**

CUM FOR ME **IV**

By **Ca$h & Company**

Available Now

RESTRAINING ORDER **I & II**

By **CA$H & Coffee**

LOVE KNOWS NO BOUNDARIES **I II & III**

By **Coffee**

RAISED AS A GOON I, II, III & IV

BRED BY THE SLUMS I, II, III

BLAST FOR ME I & II

By **Ghost**

LAY IT DOWN **I & II**

LAST OF A DYING BREED

BLOOD STAINS OF A SHOTTA I & II

By **Jamaica**

LOYAL TO THE GAME

LOYAL TO THE GAME II

LOYAL TO THE GAME III

By **TJ & Jelissa**

BLOODY COMMAS I & II

SKI MASK CARTEL I II & III

KING OF NEW YORK

By **T.J. Edwards**

IF LOVING HIM IS WRONG…I & II

By **Jelissa**

WHEN THE STREETS CLAP BACK I & II

By **Jibril Williams**

A DISTINGUISHED THUG STOLE MY HEART I II & III

LOVE SHOULDN'T HURT

By **Meesha**

A GANGSTER'S CODE

By **J-Blunt**

PUSH IT TO THE LIMIT

By **Bre' Hayes**

BLOOD OF A BOSS **I, II, III & IV**

By **Askari**

THE STREETS BLEED MURDER **I, II & III**

THE HEART OF A GANGSTA I II& III

By **Jerry Jackson**

CUM FOR ME

CUM FOR ME 2

CUM FOR ME 3

An **LDP Erotica Collaboration**

BRIDE OF A HUSTLA **I II & II**

THE FETTI GIRLS **I, II& III**

CORRUPTED BY A GANGSTA I & II

By **Destiny Skai**

WHEN A GOOD GIRL GOES BAD

By **Adrienne**

A GANGSTER'S REVENGE **I II III & IV**

THE BOSS MAN'S DAUGHTERS

THE BOSS MAN'S DAUGHTERS II

THE BOSSMAN'S DAUGHTERS III

THE BOSSMAN'S DAUGHTERS IV

A SAVAGE LOVE **I & II**

BAE BELONGS TO ME

A HUSTLER'S DECEIT I, II

WHAT BAD BITCHES DO I, II

By **Aryanna**

T.J. EDWRDS

A KINGPIN'S AMBITON
A KINGPIN'S AMBITION **II**
I MURDER FOR THE DOUGH
By **Ambitious**
TRUE SAVAGE
TRUE SAVAGE II
TRUE SAVAGE **III**
TRUE SAVAGE **IV**
By **Chris Green**
A DOPEBOY'S PRAYER
By **Eddie "Wolf" Lee**
THE KING CARTEL **I, II & III**
By **Frank Gresham**
THESE NIGGAS AIN'T LOYAL **I, II & III**
By **Nikki Tee**
GANGSTA SHYT **I II &III**
By **CATO**
THE ULTIMATE BETRAYAL
By **Phoenix**
BOSS'N UP **I , II & III**
By **Royal Nicole**
I LOVE YOU TO DEATH
By Destiny J
I RIDE FOR MY HITTA
I STILL RIDE FOR MY HITTA
By **Misty Holt**
LOVE & CHASIN' PAPER

KING OF NEW YORK

By **Qay Crockett**

TO DIE IN VAIN

By **ASAD**

BROOKLYN HUSTLAZ

By **Boogsy Morina**

BROOKLYN ON LOCK I & II

By **Sonovia**

GANGSTA CITY

By **Teddy Duke**

A DRUG KING AND HIS DIAMOND I & II

A DOPEMAN'S RICHES

By Nicole Goosby

TRAPHOUSE KING I & II

By **Hood Rich**

LIPSTICK KILLAH **I, II**

CRIME OF PASSION

By **Mimi**

<u>BOOKS BY LDP'S CEO, CA$H</u>

<u>TRUST IN NO MAN</u>

<u>TRUST IN NO MAN 2</u>

<u>TRUST IN NO MAN 3</u>

<u>BONDED BY BLOOD</u>

<u>SHORTY GOT A THUG</u>

<u>THUGS CRY</u>

<u>THUGS CRY 2</u>

<u>THUGS CRY 3</u>

<u>TRUST NO BITCH</u>

<u>TRUST NO BITCH 2</u>

<u>TRUST NO BITCH 3</u>

<u>TIL MY CASKET DROPS</u>

<u>RESTRAINING ORDER</u>

<u>RESTRAINING ORDER 2</u>

<u>IN LOVE WITH A CONVICT</u>

<u>Coming Soon</u>

BONDED BY BLOOD 2

BOW DOWN TO MY GANGSTA

KING OF NEW YORK